SET IN STONE

A Second Chance Small Town Novel

KELLY COLLINS

BOOK NOOK PRESS

Copyright © 2016 by Kelly Collins

No part of this publication may be reproduced, distributed, or transmitted in any form or by any means, including photocopying, recording, or other electronic or mechanical methods, without the prior written permission of the publisher, except as permitted by U.S. copyright law. For permission requests, contact kelly@authorkellycollins.com.

The story, all names, characters, and incidents portrayed in this production are fictitious. No identification with actual persons (living or deceased), places, buildings, and products is intended or should be inferred. All products or brand names are trademarks of their respective owners.

Dedication

Jim, Nik, Alec, and Gabby you mean the world to me.

Chapter 1

MEGAN

Three years ago, I had landed in prison for vehicular manslaughter. Today, I stood on the frigid sidewalk outside the Denver Women's Correctional Facility. For a fleeting moment, I wished I were locked up again. Was it wrong to crave the predictability of my past? The day Tyler lost his life, I'd lost a lot, too. At least I'd know how to survive when I'd been Tyler's hostage or a prisoner of the state. Today, I was stepping into a new world full of possibilities, and it scared the hell out of me.

My teeth chattered while the wind whistled across the blank slate of freshly fallen snow. With one hundred and eighty-six dollars to my name and my only outfit a prison-gifted pair of sweatpants and a long-sleeved T-shirt, I was lacking in everything except hope.

The sound of the horn hit me before the vehicle could be seen, but the minute the blue truck did a donut in front of me, my life became brighter. The girls had arrived. In seconds, the truck was turned off and Mickey and Holly were wrapped around me. Their loving arms reinforced my desire to push forward despite my dreadful circumstances. I had never been so grateful to see their goofy grins and feel their warm embrace.

"Shit, Megan, is that all they gave you to wear?" Mickey ran her hands up and down my near-frozen arms. She pulled the too big T-shirt up to cover my exposed shoulder.

"I'm no longer their problem."

For the first time in a long time, I was free. Free to choose, free to live, free to love and be loved. In all my years, I'd never been free or loved.

"Put this on."

Holly took off her jacket and draped it over my shoulders. Her warmth seeped into me like hot syrup on pancakes.

"Thank you. S…s…sorry," I chattered. "I'm such a pain."

Would I ever feel like I wasn't a scab on someone's arm? My therapist told me I had to stop the negative feedback that played in an endless loop in my mind, but I'd been programmed to feel worthless. Mom had planted the message on my eighteenth birthday, when she'd left my suitcase on the front porch with a note that said *Good luck with your life*. What mother says *Peace out* as soon as their child can no longer earn them EBT from the welfare department? The next sets of messages were *felt* loud and clear. Tyler reinforced my feelings of worthlessness each time he raised his voice and fist.

Mickey stood in front of me and pulled my chin forward, giving me no option but to look at her.

"Megan, stop it." She glowered at me while Holly looked over Mickey's shoulder with sympathy swimming in her eyes. "You're not a pain. You're a strong, independent woman. You can do this. Don't fall back into old habits." She pulled me into her arms and squeezed me tight. "We're your friends, and we'll always be here for you, whether you're a pain or not, and today you're not."

"That's right." Holly stepped to Mickey's side and looked down at my rolled up sweatpants, prison sneakers, and baggy shirt. "There's no way you're spending another minute in that hideous outfit. Mickey and I owe you Christmas presents, so let's go shopping." She clapped her hands and danced around me. Her enthusiasm was enough for the three of us.

"I have some money." I dipped my hand into my bra and pulled out the check I'd received that morning for two years of laundry service. "I don't want to be a charity case."

"Oh, shush." Holly wove her fingers through mine and pulled me toward the passenger side of the truck. "Get in. I'm freezing." She wrapped her sweater-covered arms around herself and shivered. "Today, your money isn't needed."

Once in the truck, the girls got all chatty about life at the ranch. Mickey got soft looking when she spoke of Kerrick and all he'd done for her.

"Without Kerrick and his brothers, I'd have nothing. The McKinleys saved my ranch, and I'm paying that kindness forward. You're the recipient." Mickey twisted the key to the old beat-up truck. The engine stuttered, then rumbled to life. "When you can, you'll do the same. Natalie and Robyn are getting out soon, and they'll need help, too."

The fabulous five was what we called ourselves. Who would have thought five women who came from such different walks of life could become best friends? Soon, Natalie and Robyn would be released, and I'd be the third set of arms wrapped around them. Holly draped her arm over my shoulders and pulled me to her side. In her arms, I felt safe, cozy, and valued. These were the sisters I'd never had. The family I'd always wanted.

Holly whispered against my hair, "Mickey, Kerrick, and Keagan were my saviors." She sighed her contentment. "The beginning is going to be tough, but you have a whole family here to help you pull through it."

The truck fishtailed in the snow as we powered forward and away from the prison. I didn't look back; that view was burned into my memory. My eyes focused forward, where a new life waited.

"First thing on the agenda is clothes. You can't live in sweatpants and a cotton tee." Mickey turned on the radio and started to hum along with the song that was playing softly in the background.

I sat a bit taller, feeling pride at having survived the first twenty-four years of my dreadful life. In a way, I'd been reborn the minute I stepped into the frosty afternoon air. This was the first day of my new life, and no one was ever going to bully me again.

The bleak, snow-covered landscape outside the prison turned into a neighborhood of earth-colored houses, then a highway filled with colored cars, and finally, a parking lot where bold colored stores marked the beginning of endless possibilities.

Mickey pulled the truck into a slot and killed the engine. "If we can't find it here, you don't need it." She lightly elbowed me in the side. "Let's go." Mickey pushed us forward and into the department store like her hair was on fire, and the store was the only place with water. "We have hair appointments and pedicures scheduled in an hour at the spa down the street—a gift from Kerrick. He wanted to do something special for our reunion."

Mickey practically swooned when she spoke of Kerrick. She was obviously in love—she lit up like an LED at the mention of her man.

"Tell me about your men." I looked down at Holly's wedding ring and Mickey's engagement ring. "I want to hear how a real man should treat a woman, just in case I run into one. I've been told they're a dying breed."

So many women gave their men a pass when it came to deplorable behavior, and I was no exception; I spent three years justifying Tyler's horrific conduct. How many times had I convinced myself that I deserved what I got?

"The McKinley men aren't easy, but they're good men. They work hard and play harder, but they're loyal and loving." Mickey didn't need to defend her man. It was obvious he treated her well. Hell, when she smiled, she had all her teeth. The man was obviously a gem.

"Is there a McKinley for me?"

I wanted a man who would treasure—not torture—me. Believe in me, not berate me. I'd never known good men. The string of losers who paraded through my childhood home terrified me. Mom was their main course, and they wanted me to be dessert. I spent most of my teenage years sleeping under my bed or tucked in the corner of my closet so they wouldn't find me. My adult years were spent much the same.

"Actually, on second thought, I don't want a man. They scare the shit out of me."

"You can't judge all men by the behavior of one."

"Well...there's Killian." Mickey shrugged her shoulders and kept walking. "He's the last remaining McKinley living on the ranch, but..." She stopped and appeared to consider her words. "He's..."

"Rigid," Holly blurted. "He's not for you. He's too intense, and a player to boot."

I looked from Holly to Mickey as they volleyed back and forth.

"Don't get us wrong," Mickey said. "He's a good guy, but he likes to be in charge, and the last thing you need is a man to dominate you."

Holly didn't miss a beat. "Outside of Killian, we have a sweet veterinarian named Roland. Then there's Cole and the two new ranch hands, Tyson and Greer." She rushed me toward the jeans and began to pull various sizes from the racks. "Are you a six or an eight?"

My shoulders lifted. "I have no idea. Let's try an eight. I was a ten before prison, but I've shed some pounds."

"Lots can change after three years in prison—attitudes, clothes sizes, sexual preference. Look at Natalie, she traded men for women when her options were limited." Holly held up the size eight pants and nodded.

"I'm no Natalie. I could never go there. She says she closes her eyes and envisions Ryan Gosling between her legs. I suppose she has a great imagination because Debra Watson could never be mistaken for Ryan Gosling, unless you're counting her facial hair."

I entered the dressing room, laughing. Visions of Ryan Gosling in a women's prison raced through my head. That poor man wouldn't stand a chance.

Holly followed me into the dressing room and put together outfits for me to try on. "Natalie always liked the blondes. She was dreaming of Bradley Cooper until I left." When I pulled my T-shirt over my head and let it fall to the floor, she gasped. "Oh, Megan,

I'm so sorry." Her cold fingertips traced over the scars left by cigarettes and belt buckles.

"It's all behind me," I reassured her, and it was, literally. Not a blemish could be seen on the front of me. Everything I'd endured had been delivered in a cowardly fashion—behind my back, so Tyler didn't have to see my face.

Over the top of the door, lacy bras, satin bras, briefs, hipsters, and thongs in every color rained down on me. Mickey was outdoing herself in the undergarment department. I was overwhelmed by the choices and must have looked like a deer caught by a bright light. Holly shook her head and began folding the garments.

"We'll take all of these. Try them all out and see which style suits you." She held up the black lace bra with fuchsia trim and smiled. "Someone is going to love this on you."

Mickey pulled the door open just as the soft blue material of the sweater draped over my hips. After a long whistle, she declared that I cleaned up nicely.

I turned to face the mirror. "I can't remember a time when my clothes fit." I rubbed my hands down my flat stomach. "The last time I wore street clothes, my tummy was busting out of my pants."

A tear slipped from my eye before I could wipe it away. I wrapped my arms around myself and let the tears that couldn't be contained run free.

Mickey pulled me into her arms. "That's the past, Megan. No one's asking you to forget it, but don't allow it to determine your future." She let me go, picked up the sweatpants and cotton tee I'd worn into the store, and tossed them in the nearby trash can. "This is garbage. No more garbage for you. You deserve better." She pointed to the jeans and soft tunic I was wearing. "You're wearing that out. You look like a million bucks wrapped in denim." She grabbed armfuls of clothes and rushed us toward the register. "We can't be late. Pampering awaits."

The cashier acted like a rabid dog when she found out she had to scan the tags from my body, but Mickey let it drop that my last residence was the county prison. The cashier banked her irritation and hurried us through the line like we were armed and dangerous.

I straightened my shoulders and stood tall in the cloud of Mickey's confidence. I'd never seen her so capable, and I said a silent prayer that someday I would have a fraction of her self-assurance.

Next stop was a drive-in for coffee. Who would have thought a girl could fall in love with a mocha latte? Men weren't necessary when you had chocolate and caffeine.

We entered the spa arm in arm. After my toes had been polished Tickle Me Pink, I was taken to the salon where a woman named Coco fondled my hair.

"What are we doin', darlin'?" She pulled me to the sink before I could answer. I was under a stream of hot water when she asked, "Do you trust me?"

"Um...yeah...I guess."

What did I tell a woman who was in a position to drown me? The truth was, I didn't trust anyone except Mickey, Holly, Natalie, and Robyn. I'd been burned too many times to trust blindly, but how much trust did a hairdresser require?

She brushed and clipped until layers of soft brown hair flowed over my shoulders. If I thought a mayo rinse made my hair feel soft, whatever Coco used made my hair feel like mink—and smell like watermelon on top of that.

"You like?" Coco stood behind me with a toothy grin on her face. The girls flanked her, nodding like bobbleheads on the dashboard of a speeding car.

"Yes. I love it." I wove the soft locks between my fingers. "You made me look almost pretty."

Who was this girl in front of me? I reached out to touch the mirror. She was me. I was her. We'd get through this together.

Coco shook her head. "Darlin', you were already pretty. I made your beauty shine, is all." She swiped her hands back and forth and declared, "My work is done."

In a matter of hours, I had gone from a homeless waif to an attractive woman. There was no glass slipper and no pumpkin carriage, but I had two amazing fairy godmothers.

Chapter 2

MEGAN

Mickey pulled into a long, winding dirt road. Spiky plants and scrub-oak dotted the landscape while boulders the size of small cars flanked the entrance. Beneath the large *M and M Ranch* sign swung a smaller sign that read *Second Chance Ranch*. This was it. This was my new home.

My eyes blurred with tears too great to hide. The floodgates had opened again, and I prayed each tear I shed would wash away my hurts, my disappointments, and my past.

Through the haze of my emotions, the rough outline of a large farmhouse and eight cabins stood like a welcoming committee. Mickey threw the shifter into park and hopped out.

"Let's go. I can't wait for you to see your cabin."

She pulled the bags of clothes from the back of the truck and was halfway to the front door before I slipped from the truck bench to the frozen ground.

Holly pulled me toward cabin number six. Warm wood timber and a painted red door invited me to the place where I would discover who I would become.

Wind whistled between the buildings. "You'll get used to that. I find the sound soothing," Holly said as she led me to where Mickey was seated on the front porch swing.

Mickey rose and stood behind me. "It's your house, Megan; are you going to open it up and invite us in?"

I approached the door slowly and turned the cold brass handle. Warmth from the inside rushed out. The scent of lemon swirled around me. I stood in the entry and looked at my home. *My home.*

Front and center was a fireplace with an empty mantel I'd fill with pictures of happy moments. Two chairs and a soft looking sofa waited to be tried out. I spun in a circle and saw the kitchen with its small farmhouse table, stainless steel appliances, and fancy coffee maker. Oh, how I missed the aroma of freshly brewed coffee.

Mickey disappeared down the hallway. Holly wrapped her arms around me and rested her chin on my shoulder. "Pretty awesome, right?"

"I have no words."

This was better than any place I'd ever lived. The sheer fact that the lights came on when you flipped the switch was a bonus. I couldn't count the number of times I'd done my homework by moonlight.

Mickey went straight for the fireplace. She squatted down, tented some kindling, and scrunched up some paper. "You have central heat, but a fire can be nice." She placed a metal screen in front of the fireplace and faced me. "Ready for the tour?"

I was already overwhelmed, but I nodded and followed the girls around.

"You have two bedrooms, but I imagine you'll use the closest room for yours."

We turned to the right and entered my sanctuary. I took in the beauty of the aqua and brown bedspread while I inhaled the scent of wildflowers from the candle that sat on the nightstand.

"I love it." Everything was perfect, especially the saying stenciled on the wall: *Courage is resistance to fear, mastery of fear—not absence of fear.*

"Mark Twain was a smart guy." Holly put her hand on my shoulder. "Fear is good, Megan. It helps us realize danger. Just don't let it paralyze you."

"Good advice."

"It's going to be okay," they said in unison.

After walking through the home, we ended in the kitchen, where Holly did a Vanna White flourish for my refrigerator before opening it up. The top shelf was packed full of cans of my favorite soda. The rest of the shelves were packed with everything from salami to asparagus.

The cabinets were also filled. Boxes of Lucky Charms lined the shelves. I couldn't wait to have my first bowl. Would I eat the cereal and leave the candy treasures for last, like I did as a kid, or would I eat the candy marshmallows first? No, I'd eat them together. This wasn't a box of cereal I had to protect or savor. From now on, I could eat Lucky Charms whenever I wanted.

Mickey reached into the fridge and pulled out three cans of soda. Holly and I followed her into the living room. I curled into one of the single chairs and sighed. This was a great beginning to my new life.

"This was your cabin, right?" I looked at Holly for an answer.

"Yes, for a short time, but I found I liked Keagan's cabin better." She popped the top of her soda can. "There's nothing better than a warm, naked cowboy waiting for you in bed at the end of a long day." She turned her ear toward the door. "As you can hear from the wind, the nights can be cold."

"Speaking of men," Mickey said, "Holly and I are heading out of town in a few days to meet the in-laws. It's the best time for us to go because we don't have a lot of people coming to the ranch to ride their horses, and breeding won't pick up again until spring. Are you going to be okay being alone on the ranch with the guys? If not, we can take you with us."

Being the only woman on the ranch terrified me, but being the fifth wheel on a meet-the-in-laws vacation sounded worse.

"I'll be fine." I wasn't sure that was the truth. I hadn't been around men regularly in years. Male guards didn't count. Worst case, I could hole up inside until they got back. There were enough boxes of Lucky Charms to sustain me. "I have to learn to live in this world, and the last time I looked, men are nearly half the population."

I talked the talk, but I wasn't sure how steady I could walk the walk. Natalie's voice echoed in my head: *Listen, girlfriend, fake it until you make it.*

"Tonight, you'll meet all the men from the ranch at Rick's. I can vouch for Killian, Cole, and Roland. However, Tyson and Greer are new to the ranch, and although they seem nice enough, I don't know them well enough to give my seal of approval." Mickey plopped her booted feet on the coffee table. Bits of hay fell to the surface.

"Damn it, Mickey, you're messing up Megan's floor." Holly pushed her foot toward Mickey's and forced her shoes off the table.

"She has a vacuum and plenty of time on her hands." Mickey leaned forward and brushed the hay onto the floor. "Speaking of time, meet me at my house at six. We'll head to Rick's Roost together. Maybe you'll meet someone there and run off to have wild sex. I'd totally recommend getting back in the saddle right away."

My lips twitched up. "I don't know, Mickey. I don't think I've ever truly been in the saddle."

"I'd say it's time to pull on your boots and kick up your spurs." Mickey lifted herself from the couch and walked to the front door. "Welcome home, Megan. Your clothes are in your room. You know where to find us."

Holly stood and pointed to the front door. "I'm next door if you need anything. I left books in the shelves and a list of the best TV shows on the counter." They disappeared out the door.

My heart pounded when it clicked shut. This was the first time I'd been alone in years. I often sought solitude by curling into the corner of my bunk, but it was impossible to mute the sounds of 1,100 inmates trying to be heard.

Back in the kitchen, I spent several minutes trying to figure out the coffee machine. Different flavored pods sat on the counter. Power on. Pod in. Cup in place. Start button. Like magic, a mocha latte became a reality. Although this wasn't as good as the coffee shop, from this point forward a mocha latte would always taste like freedom.

I walked circles around the living room until I stopped in front of the bookshelves filled with brightly colored covers. Lots of romance, a few mysteries, and a book called *What Now?* It was the question I'd been asking myself all day.

I pulled it from the shelf and glanced at the back cover. *Finding yourself in an uncertain world.* This would be a must-read for me, even though the hunky bare-chested guys on the bookshelf looked more interesting.

Idle hands—idle mind. Time to get busy. Once in my room, I hung up my clothes and folded my underwear. The girls were so generous. I could wear something different every day and not repeat an outfit for a week. Had there ever been a time where I'd owned so much?

After I brushed, blushed, and glossed, I pulled the self-help book from the shelf. Chapter one was about knowing yourself. Page ten had a sticky note.

Megan,

There's a pad of paper and a pen in the kitchen drawer. I found this book helpful when I got out. It helped me decide the truths of my life. Don't let someone else determine who you are. Find out for yourself.

Love,

Holly

Lost in the exercise, I was startled by the knock on the front door. "Megan, let's go." The solid wood door muffled Holly's voice.

I tucked the note back into the book, raced to the closet where I'd hung my new jacket, and whipped the door open. "S—"

Her fingers covered my lips. "There's no need for sorry."

I gave her a quick nod and yanked the door shut behind me. I locked it up tight with the keys Mickey had left behind.

Despite the potholes and spiky plants that marred our path, we arrived at Mickey's house intact. The whinny of an occasional horse and the whispering wind were the only sounds that broke the silence.

"Where are all these cowboys I've heard about?" I turned in a circle, my palms skyward. "I see nothing."

"Keagan, Cole, and Tyson are picking up supplies. Killian and Roland went to pick up a rescue, and Kerrick is at work serving and protecting. Greer is either already at the bar or somewhere around the ranch."

The peacefulness that surrounded me was a welcome respite to the constant noise in my head. It gave me space to think. "I found your book, and I got caught up in the exercise. That's why I'm late."

"Have you discovered anything about yourself?"

"Not yet, but I've only just begun."

We all piled into Mickey's truck. When the radio came on, a song about love in the back seat played while Mickey laughed. "I wouldn't recommend that." She stretched her spine and groaned. "Too hard on the back."

Minutes later, we pulled into the full parking lot of Rick's Roost.

Chapter 3

MEGAN

Holly babbled like a teen after prom. "This is a tradition. On your first night out, you have to let off some steam. They have great food, cold beer, and you'll meet the gang. The McKinley men will stop after two drinks, and they'll be the designated drivers. Everyone from the ranch is coming here to meet you, our guest of honor."

My heart thundered. "Does everyone know my crime?" How would they look at me if they knew I was responsible for two deaths, even though I was charged with only one?

When Tyler sideswiped the car, we both rolled down the embankment. He was ejected and died instantly. I was trapped, bleeding in the wreckage. My unborn child died. That would be an entry for the what-I-know-about-myself paper. I carried immense guilt over the loss of that tiny life.

"They know you served time, but I believe it's your story to tell." Mickey pulled me from the morose thoughts swimming in my head. "Kerrick knows everything because no one gets on my ranch without a background check. I gotta admire his desire to protect me and the ones I love, but don't worry, he won't say a word. Just own it. You served your time. No one will judge you."

When Mickey threw open the door of the bar, my senses were assaulted. It was far too much to digest in one glance. I focused on the smells first. French fries and burgers scented my left. Off to my right, the faint smell of men's cologne lingered in the air.

I love the musky smell of men's cologne. Another entry.

Neon bar signs cast a rainbow of color on a handsome man walking toward us. Both of his hands were full, carrying big trays of hot wings. He stopped in front of us and pressed his lips to Mickey.

"I've got the wings. Keagan is waiting on the pitchers of beer." He nodded toward a table in the corner. "Roland just got here and bought a round of shots." The man looked past Mickey to me. "I'm Kerrick. I'd shake your hand, but then we'd have no wings. Welcome home, Megan."

"Nice to meet you." My voice shrank to near silence in the big room.

"He's sexy as all hell, right?" Mickey patted the ass of her man as he passed us.

The booth was filled with big, sturdy-looking men. I took a step back and analyzed the situation. I could only see their hands, but big hands always meant big hurts.

Kerrick seemed nice enough, but I wasn't sure of the others. A blond and three dark-haired men sat in a row. I could feel the fight-or-flight response kick in. Before I could turn and flee, Mickey pushed me into the booth and sandwiched me between the blond and Kerrick. Trapped between the two men, I watched them carefully while introductions were made.

"Everyone, this is Megan. She'll be living in Holly's old cabin."

Mickey pointed to each man in order. Roland was next to me. He had a nice smile and gave off a friendly vibe. Next to him was Cole, then Greer, and finally Tyson. They all seemed welcoming and pleasant, but so was Tyler when he asked me to live with him. Sometimes a smile was what you showed the world when you were trying to hide your dark soul.

I lowered my head and whispered the words, "Nice to meet you all."

Three *thunks* hit the table. I withered into the corner of the booth. The dark-haired man delivering three pitchers of beer smiled warmly. "I'm Keagan, Holly's husband." His chest swelled as he said the words, and I wondered what would it feel like to have a man claim me with the same pride and passion Keagan felt for Holly.

Roland slid shots around the table and raised his glass to toast. "Here's to Megan and her new beginning." He warmed me with his words of welcome.

"Wait." Mickey scoured the room. "Where in the hell is Killian? We can't toast until the entire gang is here."

Seconds later, tall, dark, and dangerous approached the table.

"Killian, you're late." Mickey shoved a shot glass into the man's hand and lifted her drink in the air. "Here's to Megan."

Everyone touched glasses, tossed back the amber liquid, and then slammed the empty glasses upside down on the table. I was the only one who shivered as the alcohol burned its way from my throat to my stomach. I'd never had the opportunity to drink much, but I could see with this group, drinking was a requirement.

"The first one's the hardest," Keagan said while he poured everyone a glass of beer and climbed into the booth next to Holly. "Have a chaser. It will help the next round go down more smoothly."

The glass slipped from my hand and sloshed onto the table. I closed my eyes and flinched. "I'm sorry. I'm so sorry."

"Party foul," the deep voice sounded. "It's okay, spilled beer is obligatory in these situations. Thanks for getting it out of the way." Killian nailed me in place with his blue eyes, then lifted his beer, making sure it spilled over the side of his glass. "See?" Each person at the table followed his lead. After a good laugh, we dug into the trays of chicken wings that floated on a pool of beer.

The man the girls described as rigid and intense wasn't what I had imagined. As he stood at the end of the table, his height cast a shadow across the group. The rumble of his deep voice made the hair on my arms rise. My gut told me he was dangerous, but it was hard to consider a man who made light of my blunder a threat.

"Why so late?" Mickey asked.

Set in Stone

Killian sipped his beer. "I stopped by the ranch to drop off our new boarder. He's a feisty one. Bad attitude and stubborn aren't a good mix. Cutting off his nuts didn't seem to help with that much either." Killian then tossed his head in the direction of the stage, where a man was setting up his equipment. "I also helped Ryker bring in his stuff. He came down for open-mic night. His bar, The Nest, has run into some licensing problems."

I looked toward the man setting up an amplifier on the tiny stage. He had a don't-fuck-with-me-look. Call me crazy, but I was still drawn to the bad boys. There was something inherently sexy in those men I couldn't figure out in a glance. I'd have to make a note of that.

Need to set the bar higher for men.

I took another look around the table at the men sitting with us. Roland was easy to call. He was the kind of guy every girl should date and marry. He was clean-cut and successful, and he appeared kindhearted. I couldn't get a read on the three ranch hands. Cole and Tyson chatted about the horses and the work to be done while Greer's marble-hard eyes undressed me. I wasn't sure whether I should be flattered or fearful. The punching of my heart against my ribs told me the latter was more appropriate.

Kerrick and Keagan were in the bad boy category, too, but Mickey and Holly had tamed their hearts. Killian was a puzzle. He was as big as an oak tree, and as mean-looking as a case of the clap. However, his consideration and soft tone belied the persona I'd been led to expect. *Don't judge a book by its cover*, people said, and yet I could guarantee every book cover that contained a blood-dripping knife would have a murder inside. Nope, I was convinced that what you see is what you get.

Mickey grabbed a wing from the platter. "He's the guy from Fury, right? Didn't he do time for murder?"

"Yep, so all you jailbirds are in good company." Killian leaned across the table, stared into my eyes, and asked, "What did you go to prison for, Megan?"

Could the group hear my stomach crash to the floor? All eyes turned to me. This was the moment I hid it or owned it. I was terrified. Would they judge me? Hate me? The *swish, swish* of blood pulsing through my veins pounded like a jackhammer in my head.

I sucked in an exaggerated inhale. "I was sentenced to six years for vehicular manslaughter, but my punishment was reduced to three years in jail and then parole." The air rushed out with my words. A hush came over the table, then everyone started chatting again as if nothing shocking had just occurred. Not an eyebrow lifted. Not a head tilted.

"You should come and meet Ryker." Killian offered me his hand, but I shook my head.

"I'm good, thanks." I had to give myself credit. I was at a table filled with intimidating men, and I hadn't had a full-blown panic attack—yet. Maybe I was progressing.

After buying the second round of shots for the group, Killian left the table and stood by the man he called Ryker. I was split between listening to stories about the ranch and watching Killian get climbed by a willowy blonde dressed in short shorts and a pair of cowboy boots.

Doesn't she know it's winter?

"Megan?" A tap on my shoulder went unanswered. "Megan?" Lost in a private thought, Holly's voice rose above the din and snapped me back from the soft porn happening in the corner.

"I'm sorry. There's too much stimulation. Lots of sights, sounds, and smells rushing at me. What were you saying?"

I took one last glance at Killian. Instead of embracing the girl wrapped around his hips, he was peeling her from his body. His eyes were fixed on me. When the girl wouldn't relent, he turned her around, smacked her ass, and sent her on her way. I snapped my head toward Holly.

"I was just saying we need to get you settled before Mickey and I leave next week. Between all of us, we should have an extra cell phone to give you, and your cabin is stocked with everything you should need."

"You didn't put the monster dick in her room, did you?" Cole asked.

"What?" My attention turned to him. He was also tall and dark, but not nearly as handsome as the McKinley men.

"When Holly came to the ranch, I thought she might need a little action, so I left her a gift in her drawer." Mickey waggled her brows excessively.

"That wasn't a little action, it was the size of a donkey dick with the power of a piston." Cole shivered like he was reliving a nightmare.

"I don't know what to say to that. Not sure if I'm relieved or disappointed that there wasn't one in my drawer." I tilted my head in thought.

"I still have it."

"No, you don't." Kerrick pulled Mickey to his side. "I tossed it, baby. It intimidated me."

"You have nothing to worry about." She nuzzled into his neck.

Mickey and Kerrick canoodled next to me. Feeling a bit in the way, I asked the men to my right to let me exit. All four stood like gentlemen while I scooted around the booth.

Lights across the room flashed the word *restroom* in bold blue letters. Killian stood by the exit and tracked me until I disappeared through the swinging doors. A chill skittered down my spine. *What was wrong with me?* I'd been out of prison less than a day, and I was falling into my old habits. Fear and anxiety were bubbling under the surface. I needed to tamp it down before it took over. *Fake it till I make it. Fake it till I make it.* I checked under the stalls to make sure I was alone, then stood in front of the mirror and gave myself a pep talk.

"You've got this. You're not a victim. You're a survivor. You're strong and capable." I pinched my pale cheeks and took a deep breath before I exited the restroom and walked into a wall of muscle. "Oh, my God. I'm so sorry." I reached for my chest. Heart pounding. Breathing out of control. Dizzy. Strong hands wrapped around my arms and steadied me. I craned my neck to look into the Tiffany-blue eyes of Killian McKinley.

He gentled his grip. "Hey, it's okay. No need for apologies."

I wrenched free and stepped backward, banging my head on the wall. "Ouch." I rubbed the back of my head, easing the sting from the hit. "Are you stalking me?"

His laugh was gut-deep and full-bodied. Not the kind of laugh a person can fake, but the kind that comes from somewhere within, someplace pure and uninhibited.

"That's a new one for me. Stalked maybe, but never the stalker." He leaned in and caged me against the wall. "Do you think I'd stalk you here when you are living less than fifty yards away from me every day as my neighbor?"

I felt silly for suggesting it. "No, I imagine you don't have time to stalk women. You're too busy having girls climb up your body while you pick them off like lint."

Where did that come from?

Obviously, my courage waxed and my filter waned with alcohol consumption, or maybe I'd drawn courage from my motivational talk in the bathroom. Either way, mouthing off wasn't my norm. I'd learned the hard way to keep my mouth shut.

"Actually, Trish is a pain in my ass. She doesn't know when to quit."

He backed up against the opposite wall and folded his arms across his broad chest. The rolled-up sleeves of his shirt showed the definition of his muscled forearms. Arms capable of so much power, so much pain.

"So, you tossed her aside with a dismissive word and a smack." I emphasized the word 'smack'. It was one of those words that sounded exactly like it felt.

He shook his head the way people did when something unbelievable was mentioned. "I just wanted to make sure you were okay. Long, dark hallways and inebriated girls are a dangerous mix."

I stood up as tall as my five-foot-six-inch frame would allow. "Yeah, well, after three years in prison, I'm pretty sure I can take care of myself."

"Is that right?" He leaned forward and brushed his thumb across my lower lip. "I think it's cute that you think so."

"Asshole," I muttered under my breath as I brushed past him

and walked back into the bar. I weaved through the crowd building on the dance floor and took a place against the wall.

Ryker sang a ballad about a sparrow with eyes the color of the earth and sky while I people watched. Off to my right, Killian held up an adjacent wall and continued to stare at me. When Ryker began to sing an upbeat song, the dance floor filled fast. Mickey and Kerrick, along with Holly and Keagan, took a place in the center and swayed to the beat.

I watched Keagan pull Holly into his arms and hold her tight. He buried his head in her hair as they moved to the beat of the music. I'd never known love like theirs. My love was offered as a survival mechanism.

"Let's dance, sugar." Calloused hands pulled me from my safe space against the wall.

"No." I pulled back, but the tall, lanky cowboy was persistent. He leaned over and blew his whiskey-laced breath against my neck. "That's no way to treat a man paying you attention, doll." He wrapped his arm painfully around my waist and dragged me to the dance floor.

The bitter taste of bile rose in my throat. I'd been free for less than a day, and already some stupid asshole was intent on pushing his will on me. Never again. What was it that Robyn taught me? *One to the nose and one to the hose.* I fisted up and swung like my life depended on it and landed a solid hit to the guy's nose. My foot connected with nothing. I wanted to level the asshole, but Killian stepped into the melee. Before I knew it, I was back against the wall, watching Killian address my tormentor.

"She said no, asshole." He pulled the man's hands from his bloody nose and held his arms behind his back. "'No' fucking means 'no.' Always." The man struggled against Killian's grip. The chain that hung from his belt was removed in a flash and wrapped around the shit-faced cowboy's wrists like he was roping a steer. With a tug, Killian had him subdued and was escorting him to the door.

Moments later, he walked back to where I was glued to the wall. The chain jangled in its place at his side. I pressed myself against the wood paneling, trying to fade into the grain.

"You okay?"

I rubbed at my knuckles. "I could have finished him myself." Despite my two-shot courage, I knew that was a lie, but Killian didn't know that, and he didn't need to see my weakness.

"I was just protecting what needed protecting," he said. "I'd hate to see you back in prison. Wouldn't a bar brawl be against your parole?"

"Oh, shit." I'd be back in Cell Block C to serve more time.

"Don't worry. I convinced him to let it go. He won't be pressing any charges tonight."

I was grateful Killian had stepped in, but I couldn't be indebted to another man. Favors always came with a price. "I'll never let another man push me around or lay a hand on me. I'd kill him first."

Killian lifted his brows until they nearly touched his hairline. "Sounds like you've already ridden that stretch of road and it didn't go so well. I simply offered you a detour."

"Why do you care?" I fisted my hands and shoved them in my pockets.

"I don't, darlin', but if you don't want to travel that path again, you *should* care."

He turned and walked away, leaving me wondering who the hell Killian McKinley was.

Chapter 4

KILLIAN

Standing outside, I rolled down my sleeves and tried to get warm. What the hell was I thinking? To tell Megan I didn't care was outside the truth. She was important to Mickey and Holly, and those women were important to my brothers, Kerrick and Keagan. In a roundabout way, caring about her was requisite.

It didn't take Freud to see she was timid and scared, and although she punched the guy, she never would have done it without downing two shots of stupidity.

I read her like a large print book. She quaked in the presence of men. She flinched when she thought she would be punished. She shrank into herself when someone spoke too loud or moved too fast. She was no different from the horses I rescued. They backed away until threatened, and then they acted without thought. It would take a gentle but firm hand to gain her trust.

"There you are." Mickey led the gang out the door. "Are you good to drive?"

"Yep, I'll take Megan." I found her in the back of the crowd, looking like she wanted to disappear into the pavement. I wrapped my arm around her shoulders and led her to my truck.

"Megan," Holly called out. "Are you good with that?"

I leaned down and whispered into her hair. "You'll be fine, Megan. I'll take care of you."

Despite the quaking of her body, she turned toward her friends. "Yes, I'll be fine. It's a short drive." Her voice quivered. "See you at the ranch?"

"We'll race you there." Mickey laughed while she ran to her truck. The others scattered like mice running toward cheese.

I opened my door and helped Megan slide onto the big bench seat. Greer waited next to his truck and stared at Megan like she was a morsel to be devoured. I had no claim on her, but if she was looking for a man, he wasn't the guy for her. I'd seen him in action, and he was an asshole. There was nothing wrong with a love-them-and-leave-them attitude—I wrote that playbook—but a woman should never be left in the men's room stall while the man she just fucked moved on to the next girl.

We drove through Lone Star, which was becoming more of a luxury housing development than the ranch lands that used to take up all the acreage.

"Does your hand hurt?" I reached across the bench to take her hand in mine.

She snapped it back and tucked it against her chest. "I'm good. I didn't get as hard of a hit in as I'd have liked."

"Good enough to draw blood."

"I suppose good enough will have to suffice." Resignation was etched into each word.

The silvery glow of the full moon lit up the landscape. Spikes of yucca plants looked like sharpened blades while the fresh snow sparkled like diamonds. Sparkly and prickly, like the woman sitting near me.

"Full moon tonight. You know what they say about full moons?" I grabbed the pack of gum from the console and offered her a piece. She declined.

"The crazies are out?" She stared out the window.

"No. It's bright enough to see your future but dim enough to hide your past."

We drove under the Second Chance Ranch sign I'd carved and painted. We made our way up the long driveway. Ahead, Kerrick was helping Mickey from the truck. His hands cradled her ass as she slid down his body. What would it be like to love a woman that deeply?

In the distance, the cabins stood dark against the backdrop of land that went on for miles. The stars twinkled above, giving the scene a fairy tale effect.

"You're home, Megan." I pulled in front of cabin six and threw the gearshift into park. "I'm in cabin eight, should you need anything." I opened the door and offered her my hand.

She stared at me like I was a leper. Her untrusting eyes scanned her surroundings before she laid hers in mine and let me help her down. Once on the ground, she snapped her hand back and tucked it into her jacket pocket. Trust was something earned, not demanded. I'd earn her trust.

Greer came out of nowhere. "How about a tour of the ranch tomorrow? I can show you around."

"Negative." I stepped between them. "You have lots of work tomorrow. The fences have to be repaired in the pasture."

"Shit, man, that will take days." Greer stomped his foot like a spoiled child.

"You came here to work, right?" I stepped in front of Megan so she was positioned solidly behind me. "If not, I suggest you pack up your shit and leave. We're not a tour company. We're a working ranch, and 'work' is the key word."

Greer spun around and strode toward his cabin. He was in number four, right next to Cole, who lived in number five. Tyson had disappeared into cabin three. One and two were left vacant for the next round of ex-cons.

"Let's get you inside."

Mickey and Holly rushed past me and grabbed Megan for a hug. "We'll let you sleep in tomorrow. Roland wants to show you our pregnant mares. He says he'll knock around noon." The girls gave Megan another hug and disappeared into the shadows.

I put my hand on the small of her back. She stiffened. "You

don't have to fear me, Megan. I'm just trying to help." At her door, I backed away. She looked over her shoulder and met my gaze. Her eyes showed an array of emotions. Gratitude? Relief? Fear? I waited for the door to close before I left.

When the lock clicked into place, I hightailed it to the stables to make my rounds. I had to check on our newest boarder. Horses got scared like people did. This was a strange place to him. Strange neighbors were in the stalls beside him. I imagined it was like going to a new school on the first day.

"Hey, boy." I pulled an apple from the box on the wall. Early on in the training process, I wasn't beyond bribing. Even the most stubborn of creatures would soften long enough to get what they wanted. "You want this?" I raised the apple so the thin stream of moonlight sifting through the window would catch it just right. "Yes, I know you do."

The horse stood in the corner of the stable and showed me his ass until I bit into the apple. He glanced over his shoulder and dismissed me again.

"Playing hard to get? That's okay. I'm patient, but you need to know I always win, and soon you'll be eating out of my hand."

I broke the apple up into pieces and tossed it to the floor before I walked away. I could hear the crunch of him chewing while I walked out of the stables.

It was funny how my life changed course the moment I moved here. I had one goal when I'd arrived, and that was to make M and M Ranch a success. If I plowed forward, I'd be able to achieve my goal in short order. My definition of success was simple: be in control of everything, from your finances to your dick. I was succeeding in the former; the latter, I was working on.

I walked into my cabin and straight to the refrigerator. The beer spilled over the bottle when I popped the cap, reminding me of the sheer terror I saw on Megan's face when she spilled her beer on the table. What the hell was her real story?

The cushions gave when I plopped on the sofa, curling around my body like a hug. I glanced around my cabin.

Yep, I love it here.

Whips hung from my walls. I showcased them like fine art. Each one represented a moment in my life that helped define me as a man. I knew what people thought of me. People believed what they wanted, and I let them. It worked to my advantage.

Chapter 5

MEGAN

Alone in my cabin, I locked the door and checked all the windows. It seemed as if I'd spent my life locking myself away. I walked twice around my space, making sure I didn't miss something.

I picked up my pen and jotted down the things I knew for certain.

I like men's cologne.
I don't like whiskey.

I thought about the guy who tried to manhandle me onto the dance floor and made a final note.

Men can't be trusted.

Killian was different, though. He was strong but soft. Big but non-threatening. His nearness made me nervous, and yet somehow he comforted me.

Killian isn't what he seems.

I shook my head and tossed the pen to the side. The biggest thing I'd learned about myself tonight was that I didn't know much about me. I only knew the girl people told me I was, and if I was ever going to get a chance at living, I was going to have to figure myself out—and soon.

The one thing I knew with certainty was that I was exhausted and crawling into my new bed was exactly what I wanted right then. After checking the doors and windows one last time, I collapsed into the softness of the mattress.

Lying in the dark, I listened intently, trying to acclimate to my new surroundings. In the distance, I heard the howl of a coyote and whir of the wind as it passed between the cabins. The faint clinking of a chain lulled me into a sound sleep.

The peacefulness of the evening conflicted directly with the commotion of the morning. The sound of horses and hoofbeats filled my room. When I bolted upright, I half-expected to see a stampede of horses blaze a trail across my bed.

I slid out of the warm covers and into yesterday's clothes. After a peek out of each window, nothing appeared out of place, so I padded my way to the kitchen and made a cup of coffee. It was only five-thirty, and if this was when every day started around the ranch, I was going to need lots of coffee.

From the back bedroom, I had a clear view of the staff stables. I sat on the spare bed and watched Cole and Tyson pull horses from their stalls to run free in the fenced area. I didn't know much about horses except they pooped a lot and the stalls needed cleaning every day. About thirty minutes later, Cole dumped a wheelbarrow of horse poop on the growing pile outside. Did I imagine it, or did my cabin smell like musty hay? Did a person get used to that smell? I imagined I'd have to eventually.

After two bowls of Lucky Charms and three episodes of *Jeopardy*, I showered and put on clean clothes. The morning had evaporated, and Roland would be knocking soon. If I had my way, I'd never leave this cabin. Here I had some semblance of control, but I promised Robyn to try everything twice before I made a final decision on anything.

"Don't try. Trying opens the chance of failure," she had said, "just do."

Determined to get my life on track, I pulled my hair into a ponytail and threw on my jacket. When Roland came calling, I'd be ready. It was time to push myself out of my comfort zone.

"Hey," Roland said as he approached. "I thought I was going to have to roust you out of bed. You looked beat last night."

"I was tired, but apparently sleep is optional at a ranch. Do they always start before the sun rises?"

"Ranch life is hard." Roland offered his hand. "Killian runs a tight ship here, but it works because everyone knows the expectations." When I didn't take his hand, he nodded toward the stables and walked in that direction.

"I thought Mickey ran things?" I double-timed my steps to keep up with him.

"Oh, she does, but she realized she had to delegate. She gives riding lessons and takes care of the tack. She turned over the training to Killian, the breeding to Keagan, and I make sure the animals are healthy."

We arrived at the big stables and walked past stalls of horses. They came in every color and size. There was even a tiny horse Roland assured me was full-grown.

"He's the meanest horse here. He bites."

"I never imagined horses to be biters."

I glanced over the stall at the tiny tan horse. When he rushed forward, I stumbled back and would have landed on my ass if Roland hadn't caught me.

"Easy there." He righted me and let me go. "Until they know you, you want to approach slowly and with caution. Do you want to meet the girls? I'm doing an ultrasound on Sunset."

I felt a little giddy going to meet the pregnant horses. "Is there a problem with Sunset?"

"I'm not sure yet. She's just over four months along, but her foal isn't thriving like the others. The umbilical cord is twisted, and the pass-through of nutrients isn't optimal."

Roland stopped at the end stall and clucked. A beautiful russet-colored horse came straight to him and rubbed his head with her muzzle.

"Come here." He motioned me over, placed my hand on her forehead, and began to coo to the horse.

"Hey, girl, how's that foal of yours?"

The horse tossed her head and swished her tail in reply. After placing a lead over Sunset's head, Roland led her out of the stall. We walked on her left all the way to the barn, where he slid her into a narrow metal shoot.

"This smaller area is to protect her and me. She's less likely to kick." He pulled an enormous glove from a box in the cupboard and pulled out a monitor. "You're going to be my assistant today." He plugged in the monitor, and it flickered to life.

"Surely, you don't need a glove that long." The rubber glove went all the way to his shoulder.

"Watch and learn." After putting a glob of lube on his hand, he pressed into the horse's rectum until he was past his elbow. "Her uterus is firm and feels healthy, but let's see how this little filly is doing."

"It's a girl?" After talking horses with Mickey for a year, I knew a few things.

"Hand me the wand."

He took the wand and palmed it before his arm disappeared again. The screen flashed with images that looked alien to me, but when I saw the frown on Roland's face, I knew things weren't what he wanted to see.

"Not good?" I felt the tears reach my eyes, and I blinked them back.

"The same." Roland freed his arm and removed the glove. After cleaning the equipment, he pulled up photos he had taken during the procedure. "See this?" He pointed to a hazy tube-like thing. "Right here where it narrows is the twist, and there isn't a damn thing I can do." Resignation was etched in the furrows of his brow. Silence shrouded us while we walked Sunset back to her stall.

"What will happen?" My heart broke for the horse, for Mickey, and the others who were waiting anxiously for the birth.

"Nature has a way of taking care of developmental issues, and this belongs in that category. I would bet the cord is too long, allowing it to twist and wrap around the fetus." He walked to the sink to wash his hands. "I'm starving. Want to get some lunch?"

The man was just elbow-to-ass in a horse, and he was hungry? "No, I'm good."

"Nonsense, I know where they have the best fried chicken. Let's go." He was a few steps ahead of me when Killian appeared.

"Megan." He pulled his Stetson off and tipped it toward me. "Are you hungry? I was just going to make some sandwiches. Care to join me?"

My heart took off like a racehorse at the derby. "Um...no, but thanks. I'm going with Roland for chicken."

His eyes widened briefly. "If he's taking you to Dinah's, get the garlic fries." Killian spun on his heel and walked toward the barn.

I swear I saw something that looked like disappointment flash across his face. *Surely not.* Rather than rush to meet up with Roland, I stared at Killian's back until he disappeared through the red-hinged doors. I wanted to run after him, but that didn't make sense.

"Are you coming?" Roland called from the truck. "I'm hungry."

I rushed to the truck and hopped in. "Don't you think it's strange having your arm up a horse's patootie makes you hungry?" I couldn't believe I was having this conversation with a man, and it felt comfortable. Roland felt safe, like I imagined having a big brother would feel.

"It's a lot of work." He flexed his muscle. "Feel this arm. It takes a lot of strength to do what I just did. I suppose maybe I should have saved the palpating for a second date."

"Wait, we're on a date?" I turned to the side and faced him. "How did that happen without me knowing?"

He shrugged. "Mickey and Holly seem to think we're a perfect match. I'm happy to see where it goes."

I pressed myself into the door. "Roland, you're a nice guy, but I've been out of prison for twenty-four hours, and I come with a lot of baggage."

"Hearing 'you're a nice guy' is always the kiss of death. Well... you have to eat, right? There's no harm in enjoying a meal together."

We pulled into Dinah's. It was straight out of a '50s movie with its cracked vinyl booths, records decorating the wall, and a jukebox in the corner. We took a seat in a center booth across from one another. When the waitress came for our order, I took Killian's advice and ordered chicken and garlic fries. Roland went for chicken and mashed potatoes. After I spent fifteen minutes trying to convince the sweet veterinarian I didn't need a puppy or a kitten, our food arrived.

I picked at my food. Thoughts of Sunset losing her filly gutted me. My appetite was gone. I didn't know if horses had motherly instincts that kicked in. Once I'd found out I was carrying, I did everything to ensure my baby was healthy, but in the end I'd still failed to protect my child.

Roland picked up a steaming piece of chicken. "What's wrong? You seem sad."

I swiped at the tear that ran down my face. "She's going to lose her baby, isn't she?"

"Most likely, but the same movement that twisted her up can untwist her. All we can do is watch, wait, and hope."

The rest of lunch was filled with innocuous questions and answers. Things like favorite movies, music, and food. I learned a bit about myself at lunch.

I love garlic fries.
I hate that Sunset's foal is at risk.
I'm not the least bit attracted to Roland.

When we pulled up in front of the barn, Killian was bare-chested and glistening with sweat. He picked up hay bales like they weighed nothing, stacking them three high and ten deep.

Outside Roland's truck, I stood and stared at Killian. He didn't acknowledge our arrival, just kept working while I kept watching. Muscles rippled with each movement. His stomach appeared as tight and strong as steel. I ached to wipe the bead of sweat that ran down his forehead. *Bad idea.* I reminded myself that many bad things started with men: menstruation, menopause, and mental illness, to name a few. I continued the list in my head—meningitis, menacing—but damn if I didn't get too distracted by the stallion tattoo etched into his chest to think of more.

Roland came into focus. "Hey, where did you go?" He stood in front of me with his head tilted. "You forgot your leftovers."

I exhaled loudly. "Sorry, I get lost in my thoughts sometimes." I took the box from his hand. The smell of garlic caught on the wind. "Thanks for lunch, Roland." Out of character, I tiptoed up and gave him a quick peck on the cheek. I was trying to find a men-word without a negative meaning when the word *mend* filled my head and heart. Yes, I would mend.

Killian grabbed the T-shirt he had tucked in his back pocket and wiped the sweat off his face before tossing it on a bale of hay and stalking toward me. "Are those garlic fries I smell? Did you bring that for me?" His smile disarmed me, and I fumbled the box, catching it just before it hit the dirt.

"No, they're my leftovers, but you're welcome to them." I reached out to pass off the Styrofoam container.

"Can you hold on a second?"

"Sure."

I walked toward the hay and laid the box on top. With Killian around shirtless, there was a high likelihood of me slipping on my drool and dumping the food. I had sworn off men for life, but no one told my girl parts. They twisted and ached at the sight of him. I wanted to run to my cabin and hide, but the cowboy in front of me drew me in. Every movement made the horse tattooed on his chest gallop. His muscles became the horse's, and every shift of his body brought it to life.

Killian walked to Roland, and I heard snippets of their conversation, phrases like "not good," "still twisted," and "too small." Killian's broad shoulders slumped forward. He pulled off his Stetson and ran his fingers through his hair, leaving it deliciously messy when he shoved the hat back on his head.

"All right. We'll just watch and see," Killian said while Roland turned and began to walk away. "Hey, don't you think your date should be walked to her cabin?"

"Not my date." Roland smiled in my direction. "She played the 'nice guy' card."

Set in Stone

Killian howled with laughter. "That's harsh, man." He looked at me and back to Roland. "You need a Band-Aid?"

"Fuck off." Roland opened the door to his truck. "Megan, check on Sunset for me, will you? She likes you." He climbed into his truck, cranked the engine, and drove away.

My cheeks were hot despite the crisp breeze that blew between us.

"You may have broken his heart." Killian raised his hand and moved toward me.

I turned my head and sank against the hay.

"Megan, I was just reaching for your leftovers."

I peeled my eyes open and saw he had the box in his hand.

He opened the box and picked up some fries. "Come here and sit down. No one likes to eat alone." Killian spoke with authority. He was the kind of man who expected people to do as he bid. His strength was obvious. Confidence and control seeped from every pore of his body.

I tried to hop up on the hay bales now stacked two high but couldn't clear the top. "Old habits are hard to break."

"Can I help you up?" He put the box to the side and held out his large hands.

I wanted to say yes. I wanted to say no. Instead, I said nothing and nodded.

He pressed his hands to my sides and lifted me with the same ease he lifted hay.

"Thank you."

He tilted his hat to me and smiled. "You are most welcome, ma'am."

I was so close to his chest. I reached out and touched the ink that created the flowing mane of the brown horse.

"Did that hurt?" My fingers lingered longer than I intended. In fact, I never expected to be so bold.

He reached up, grasped my hand, and drew it down his chest until it sat cradled on his thigh.

"I like the feel of getting a tattoo. It's painful, but there's a fine line between pleasure and pain. Some pain is worth it." He released my hand and dipped back into the box for more fries.

"I've heard lots of people say there is a fine line between pleasure and pain. I can't see it." I closed my eyes and watched the reel of my life in fast forward. "Pain is pain."

Chapter 6

KILLIAN

I pulled a block of hay from the pile and sat in front of Megan. It was a rarity that I gave up my position of power, but seeing her cower as I reached for the food was eye-opening. Perched below her, I spoke softly.

"Roland says you played the 'nice guy' card on your first date?" I was famished from moving hay bales all morning. I pulled a chicken leg from the box and chewed off a piece.

She lifted her head to look at me. "I had no idea it was a date. I don't have...I wasn't expecting...oh hell." She covered her face with her shaking hands. "I don't have good experiences with men."

I reached up to brush the hair that had fallen in front of her eyes. Happiness, fear, sadness, and affection. Everything was in the eyes. The minute I saw affection in a woman's eyes was typically the time I let them go. To lose my heart would be to lose control. There was no risk of having to cut and run with Megan; her eyes were devoid of affection and filled with terror.

"Look at me." I knew the clip of my voice scared her. The snap of her head toward me told me everything. "Megan, I won't hurt you. No one here at the ranch will hurt you."

She lowered her head. "I want to believe that."

Taking a chance, I stood and gently lifted her chin. "I promise." I didn't let her go until the fear left her eyes. "Let's try something out." I dropped my hand and took my seat again.

She cocked her head with a look of skepticism. "What?"

"It's an experiment." I tossed the leg bone into the box and wiped my mouth with the back of my hand. "We're going to be friends, and friends keep friends safe. But friends are also honest with each other, so I want you to tell me whatever comes to your mind. So…for example, if I move too fast toward you and it scares you, just yell 'scared.' I want you to find your voice. You have the freedom to speak…to be you. Okay?"

She hopped off the hay. "That's the problem. I've never been me, and I don't know who I am."

I stood slowly and tugged my shirt over my head. The breeze was kicking up, and the cold stung my skin. "Let's find out, then. In the meantime, there's someone I'd like you to meet."

I didn't reach for her. I walked ahead and hoped she'd follow me into the stables. In stall number five was our newest addition. I knew Megan trailed behind me. I felt her presence like an incoming storm. A prickle of energy charged the air around her.

I stood aside and let her approach. "This is Devil. He came here yesterday, just like you. He's scared and uncertain, just like you. It will take him time to acclimate to his new life, but I can guarantee you it's going to be better than he's had."

After realizing I held no bribe, the horse turned and showed us his backside. Megan gasped. I knew it would be shocking, but I knew deep in my soul she would understand this horse better than anyone.

"He's so scarred. Who would do that to him?" She grasped the wooden gate.

"A coward." I watched for her reaction. She white-knuckled the stall gate, and I second-guessed my decision until she spoke.

"I can't imagine him doing anything to deserve this." She stared at Devil's backside, and I swear she was counting the lashes in his hide. Her face twisted like she felt each blow the whip had delivered.

"Megan, please look at me." Megan released the gate and

Set in Stone

turned her sad eyes my way. "I can't imagine you ever doing anything to deserve what happened to you. I'm here if you need an ear." I looked around at the twenty-two stalls. "They're here, too. They're really good listeners. Shall we see how Sunset is doing?"

She followed me to Sunset's stall, but her eyes drifted back to Devil. "Can he be saved?"

I considered her question for a minute. It was a loaded question. I saw hope and fear, a second of resignation, and then something that looked like determination. "We can all be saved. The question is…how much do you want it?"

Sunset broke the tension with a nudge to Megan's shoulder. "Wow, why did she do that?"

"She's saying hello. She remembers you from this afternoon. Horses never forget. You want to make her really happy?"

"Yes, yes, I do."

I pointed to the bin on the wall. "Get her a treat. She deserves one. She had anal with Roland today. I'd say that's worth an apple, don't you think?"

After the initial shock of my statement, she laughed, and it was a beautiful sound.

"You're so bad." She studied me and waited for a reaction.

"You have no idea how bad I can be, but I hear you don't like the nice guys. Bad boys float your bo—?" She moved to the bin before I could finish my sentence. Escape and evade. I liked that game, too.

She approached cautiously with the apple. "Do you feed it to her whole?"

"You can, and she'll chew it up, but you have to think of them like children, and a whole apple is a choking hazard, so I generally bite some off or cut it in pieces." I pulled my pocket knife out and flicked it open, quartering the apple.

"Do they bite?"

I opened my hand to show her a scar on the side of my finger where a horse had nipped me good. "Yep, some do. Sunset doesn't. I wouldn't advise feeding Devil by hand until he settles down, but she's fine." I reached for her palm, and she set it in my hand. *Progress.* "Hold your hand flat and offer her the apple."

Megan squealed with delight when Sunset lipped at her hand to get the sweet apple. "It tickles." She placed another piece in her palm and grinned. When she was finished, she held her slobbery hands out like she'd contracted a disease. "Oh my God, that was fun and gross."

I grabbed a handful of hay and rubbed it between her hands to remove Sunset's gift.

"It's fun until someone loses a finger. Be careful with the other horses until they get to know you. Okay?"

"Okay."

"I have to get back to work, but it was fun, Megan. Come out to the stables whenever you want. I'll put you to work."

"Thanks." She turned around and started walking away, and the stables seemed empty despite the twenty-two horses that occupied every stall. "Hey, Killian?"

She stopped next to Devil's stall. "Don't you think he should get a nicer name? What did they expect him to act like with a name like Devil?"

I looked at the black horse. "What would you name him? Please don't say something like Daisy."

She smiled. "What's wrong with Daisy? That happens to be my favorite flower."

I shook my head. "But he's a boy."

"What about Lucky?"

"Lucky he is. All right, you've just performed your first official job as my assistant. I'll expect you in the stables tomorrow by six." I turned my back and walked toward the door.

"But—"

"No buts. We're a working ranch, not a day spa. See you tomorrow."

Chapter 7

MEGAN

At ten to six, I was walking across the field to the stables, thinking I'd beat Mr. Let's-Be-Friends to work. Nope, he was already leading a horse out to the open area.

"Didn't think you'd come." He pulled the lead off the white mare and let her loose.

"I didn't think I had much choice." I shoved my hands in my pockets and kicked at the hay under my feet. "You don't sound like the kind of man I want to disappoint."

He approached, standing just inches in front of me. I could barely breathe. Yesterday I reached out to touch him, but today I wanted to turn and run. How could I move forward if I never stood my ground? Deep inside, I knew Killian would never hurt me; now, if I could just convince my brain...

"Are you scared of me, Megan?" He reached out and gently gripped my shoulders.

He told me to say what was on my mind. Did he mean it? "Terrified." I waited for him to shake me near to death, but he didn't. He pulled me to his chest and hugged me. The scent of his cologne washed over me. He smelled like citrus and musk, fresh but sexy.

"Thanks for being honest." His chin rested on my head. "You're safe here." He took two steps back and pointed to the empty stall. "Have you ever mucked out a stall?"

Feeling more relaxed than I had in a long time, I let down my guard. "No, but anything that's called mucking can't be all that exciting." I walked into the stall and looked around. Horse poop everywhere. *Super.*

"You're going to love this." He picked up the water bucket and set it outside the stall, then handed me a rake with wide-set tines. "Scoop up the manure and put it in the wheelbarrow. We have twenty-two stalls to clean." He pushed the wheelbarrow closer. "I'll be back in a few to check on you." He twisted in his boots and walked out, leaving me alone. Well, not completely alone; there were twenty-one horses happy to watch me pick up their poop.

When the stall floor was clean, I pushed the wheelbarrow outside toward the big pile of manure.

"Done already?" Killian approached from behind. "Let me take care of that." He took the half-full wheelbarrow and turned it over like it weighed nothing. "Follow me."

I stepped in line behind him and followed like a soldier. My fear of him had turned into something else. I was no longer afraid he'd beat me; I was afraid I'd disappoint him, and that scared me more.

In front of Sunset's stall, I watched Killian put a lead over her head and walk her out. "She's so beautiful. It breaks my heart that her baby is struggling to survive. I'm sure you've seen it happen before, but do you ever get numb to it?"

"Take her lead." He guided me to her left side and handed me the leather leash. We walked side by side to the open corral. "I've seen it happen a few times, and no, I never get used to it." He showed me how to remove the lead and told me which horses would play nicely together.

For the next two hours, Killian and I worked side by side in silence. The quiet was comforting. I'd never spent time with a man who didn't constantly talk or yell.

"There you are." Holly leaned against the rail, looking at the horses. "What are you doing out here?"

I looked at Killian. "He recruited me for the morning shift."

"Are you here to steal her away? We have about ten stalls left." Killian wound the leather lead around his hand and snapped the trailing tail of it against the fence.

I jumped back and shouted. "Scared!"

Holly twisted her head and dropped her jaw.

"Oh, Megan…I'm sorry." Killian let the lead drop to the ground and stepped in front of me. "I wasn't thinking." He looked in my eyes, and all I saw was concern. "Forgive me?"

I shook off the tension and nodded.

"Megan, are you okay?" Holly's voice broke through the private moment Killian and I were sharing.

I got lost in his eyes and nearly forgot Holly was there. "Yes. Old fears are hard to put to rest, but Killian is trying to help."

Holly eyed him for a minute. Sarcasm coated her words. "I bet he is. Come on, we have to get to the DMV so you can take your driving test."

"What?" I stepped back. "I can't take a driving test. I haven't even studied."

Killian leaned against the fence, his arms crossed over his chest with one boot on the lower rail. Did he ever look anything but confident and in charge?

"It won't be much different from the first time you took it."

"Holly, I've never had a driver's license."

Holly shook her head. "How's that even possible? You were convicted of a driving crime."

I let out a breath and a growl. "You don't have to have a license to drive a car. It doesn't take a genius to turn the key and put the car in drive. I did what I had to to survive."

"Okay then, change of plans. We'll go to the DMV to get you a handbook and then off to the phone store to get this activated." She pulled a phone from her back pocket. "Let's go." With her arm over my shoulder, she led me away from the corral.

She looked behind us at Killian. "Looks like you picked up a new job."

"What's that?" He kicked off the fence and walked forward.

"Driving lessons."

"Oh, shit." He stumbled a bit, like he'd tripped over his slackened jaw.

Holly laughed the whole way to her Jeep. Once we were inside, she twisted in her seat and gave me a tell-me-everything look. "Spill."

"What?"

"What's going on with you and Killian? What happened to Roland?"

"Nothing. I had lunch yesterday with Roland, and he was nice. Would have been nice to know we were on a date."

"Oh no. You guys were perfect for each other, and you played the 'nice guy' card."

"What the hell is the 'nice guy' card?"

"You know—when you tell a guy, 'you're nice, but…'"

"Oh my God…I did that to him." I bit at the hangnail on my thumb. The cold air had dried my skin to the texture of a cracker. "He's a nice guy, but I'm not attracted to him."

She looked past me toward the stables. "You're attracted to Killian?" She opened her car door. "Follow me."

I slipped from the seat and followed her to Killian's cabin. "What are we doing here?"

She tiptoed to the front of his cabin. "I just want you to see what he appears to be into so you can make a smart decision." She took my arm and pulled me to the front window. "Look at his wall art."

Hanging like trophies were whips of every size, shape, and color. "What the hell?"

"Care to know how one of those feels as it connects to your ass?" Holly turned around and walked back to her Jeep.

I stood there and stared at the whips. Five of them hung in a row. The leather on the handle was worn from what could only be years of use. Somehow, I couldn't see Killian taking a whip to anything, and then I remembered the way the lead snapped across the fence today. My heart raced as fast as my feet, all the way back to the Jeep.

"You're quiet," Holly commented when we finished at the phone store.

"You just told me the nicest guy I've met at the ranch has the capacity to take a whip to me. How am I supposed to react to that?"

"Killian isn't going to hurt you. I'm just saying he has a reputation for liking a certain kind of sex. I imagine he's the tie-you-up-and-make-you-beg kind of man. If that's what you want, then go for it, but given your history, I don't see you willingly bending over his knee."

"I'm not looking for a boyfriend, Holly. I'm just looking for a way to live in a world with men, and Killian has been nice to me. He challenges me to get in touch with my feelings, to speak when I'm feeling threatened. When I do, he reassures me I'm allowed to have a voice."

"Oh, so that's what that was about. Good on him. He's a psychology major, in case you didn't know. I've always thought it was a weird degree for a horse trainer. He seems to like his horses more than people."

"I can't fault him. I like his horses more than people, too."

We went to the bank to set up an account, hit the DMV for a handbook, and stopped by the store so I could get more milk. The girls were leaving tomorrow, and I had boxes of Lucky Charms to devour.

It was well past lunch when we got back to the ranch. I turned the corner to my cabin and came face to face with Greer.

"Hey, I was just coming to find you. Dinner tonight, my cabin—six." His voice wasn't particularly friendly; it was demanding, but in a way that wasn't sexy like Killian's.

"Thanks for asking, but no, thanks."

He leaned in. "I could show you a good time." He trailed his fingers down my arm. "How long has it been since you've had a really good time?" His coffee breath made me want to gag.

I wanted to scream something out, but I couldn't pinpoint the emotion I was feeling. Fear? Disgust? Killian appeared like a ghost and stood between Greer and me.

"Relief," I whispered.

"Create some space, or I'll create the space I'm comfortable with, and you won't like my methods."

"Shit, man, I was just being hospitable." Greer stepped back when Killian reached for the chain at his belt. Greer looked at Killian's hand and shuffled back. "I'm leaving." He turned and disappeared around the corner.

"Stay clear of him. I don't trust him. I'd get rid of him if I didn't need the help right now, but one more slip and he's gone." Killian pressed his hand to my back and guided me up the stairs to my cabin.

"Thank you."

"You're welcome." He reached up and wiped something from my cheek. "Dust," he said.

Though his nearness should have sent my senses spiraling out of control, there was something solid and comfortable with him so close. "Did you need something, Killian?" The warmth of his hand seeped through the layers I was wearing, heating me from the outside in.

"Nope, just making sure you knew to be in the stables at six tomorrow morning."

"I'll be there."

I never thought scooping horse poop would excite me, but I'd be damned if I wasn't looking forward to working out my frustrations next to Killian. After seeing the whips hang in his home, I should have been scared to death, but I couldn't wrap my brain around him being anything but a good man.

Yes, but you thought Tyler was a good man, too.

Chapter 8

MEGAN

At five-thirty, I rushed out to say goodbye to Holly and Mickey. They were packing the last of their stuff in Keagan's truck for their trip to Wyoming.

"The big house is open if you need anything." Mickey pulled me into her arms and squeezed. "Are you going to be okay?"

"I'm a big girl, Mickey. I'll be fine." What choice did I have? I was twenty-four, and I had to look after myself.

Killian walked out of his cabin and toward us.

"What's this about being fine?" He looked over all of us, but his eyes paused on me. "Yep, I'd say you're all pretty damn fine." His heart-stopping smile fell on me.

His comment was met with a dirty look from both of his brothers. "Call us if you need anything," Kerrick said.

"Give everyone my love." Killian sidled up next to me. "Ready?" His spearmint breath whispered across my hair and caused a shiver to skitter across my skin.

"Oh yes, I've been dreaming about shoveling shit all morning." I pushed against his shoulder, then froze.

"You push like a girl." Killian threw his arm over my shoulders and walked me toward the stables. "Are you going to let me talk to you like that?"

I gave him a wary glance. I was out of my element here. I was the 'yes' girl. *You're a loser—yes. You're fat—yes. You're worthless—yes.* Killian wanted me to fight back. "I *am* a girl—I push like a girl."

"Fair enough." He never dropped his arm from my shoulders, and although the gesture was new to me, it felt good. "Have you ever ridden a horse?"

I shook my head.

"Talk to me, Megan." He stopped and turned me to face him. "I like your voice, I want to hear your words." His hands held my shoulders, giving me no room to move, and I didn't feel the need to escape his grasp.

"No, I've never ridden. Girls like me didn't get the opportunity to spend time doing things like riding horses." His grip eased, giving me the opening to step away, but I didn't. I stood a breath away from him, testing my boundaries where men were concerned.

"Girls like you? What does that mean?" He locked his arm in mine, and we began to walk again.

"Poor girls. Girls whose mothers would rather buy a pack of smokes than feed their kids. Girls who showed up to the soup kitchen because their moms would disappear for days on end and there was nothing to eat. And you know what? Those were the good days." I didn't mean to share so much of myself, but Killian was beginning to get under my skin. He had a way of breaking down my barriers.

His hand fisted. I quickened my pace, hoping to get to the stables and get started.

"You want to talk about it?"

"Not really." The stables smelled of hay and horse musk. Tails swished, and neighs filled the air.

Killian inhaled deeply. "Smells like home."

I crinkled my nose. "You need to get a housekeeper if your house smells like this." I pulled the wheelbarrow from the corner and started toward stall twenty-two.

Two hours later, I was pulling loose the skin that had blistered and broken on the pad of my thumb.

"Let me see that." He opened my fisted palm. "You'll live, but why aren't you using the gloves?" He pointed to the space above where the wheelbarrow was stored. No less than ten pairs of gloves hung unused.

"You weren't wearing any, and those aren't mine."

Releasing something that sounded like a growl, he stalked over to the wall and pulled a pair of gloves free. "Use these." He spread his palm out in front of me. "Feel my hands, Megan. They're calloused and weathered from years of work." He pulled my hand and laid it atop his palm. "Your hands are delicate and soft, and I'd like to keep them that way." He raised my palm to his mouth and blew air on the stinging blister. "Follow me." His voice was deep and stern.

Like a trained dog, I trotted behind him to a small room in the back of the stables. When we entered, he flipped the switch, and an open bulb hanging from the ceiling crackled to life.

Wooden horses held saddles and pads; pegboards held leads and everything else I imagined a horse ranch would need. He picked up a whip from the corner, and panic set in. My mind raced to recall what transgression would deserve such a punishment.

"Panicked," I yelled, hoping he meant what he said about revealing my emotions.

He looked at the whip in his hand and frowned. Slowly, he leaned it against the corner and opened the cabinet where the weapon had been propped. The first-aid kit sat in the center of the middle shelf.

"Come here." He sat on an empty wooden horse and rummaged through the box. When I hadn't budged, he said, "Please." I took the hand he offered and shuffled closer to him.

After applying some soothing cream and a Band-Aid, he released my hand, but not before kissing my injury.

"Thank you." I pulled my hand back and tucked it into my jacket pocket.

"Hungry?"

"Starved, but what about the horses?" Half the stalls were left.

"Cole and Tyson will be thrilled there are only twelve left."

"What do you mean?"

"We've been helping them since I sent Greer to the fences." It was a matter-of-fact statement.

"You don't normally clean stalls?"

"Darlin', I do whatever has to be done. That's the way of it on a ranch. Generally speaking, I don't clean a lot of stalls. I'm usually exercising the horses and retraining our rescues."

"Oh."

"Besides, I wanted to get to know you."

My heart skidded to a grinding halt. "You did? Why?"

"We're friends, and it seemed like the neighborly thing to do." He walked out of what he called the tack room and headed in the direction of his cabin. "You have a habit of saying no, so I'm going to tell you right now it's not going to be an acceptable answer. I'd like to take you to breakfast, and then to the supply store. I need a few things for Lucky."

How could I say no to a man who changed the name of a horse for me? "Okay."

His eyes widened. "Okay?" His smile heated the cold space. "All right, then. Meet me at the black truck in five. I'll tell Cole we're leaving."

WHEN GREER DROVE past me in a golf cart filled with barbed wire and steel rods, his expression was blank, but his eyes ate me up. I knew that look. I'd seen it on a hundred men's faces as they passed through my childhood home looking for a good time.

I pressed myself against the cool black metal of the truck and watched him disappear behind the barn.

"Ready?"

"Um, yes. I'm ready." I was so ready to get off the ranch and away from the other men.

Killian climbed into the truck and sat for a minute, as if in deep thought. "I'm proud of you, Megan." He turned the key, and the engine purred to life. His truck was so much smoother than Mickey's.

"Proud of me? Why?" What did I do to make this man proud?

"You're stepping out of your comfort zone. That's big."

"You said I didn't have a choice."

"True, but if you did, would you have chosen differently?" He put the truck into drive, and we moved forward.

Would I have chosen differently? "No, I would have come for you." Killian lifted his eyes at my word choice.

"Really? Now that sounds more interesting than breakfast and a trip to the supply store."

Without thinking, I reached over and punched him in the arm. "You're so bad."

He smiled in that way guys who knew they were hot did—a slow pull of his lower lip through his teeth, followed by a heated smile. "Oh, you have no idea."

He was right. I had no idea. Would I ever find out? There was something enticing and terrifying about that notion. "So…tell me something about you, Killian. I know nothing except that you're rigid and stiff."

"Wow, my reputation precedes me." Killian pounded his hands on the steering wheel and laughed. "You haven't been close enough to experience how stiff I can be." He glanced at my dropped-jaw expression. "Close your mouth. You're giving me impure thoughts."

"Oh, shush. Why are you teasing me so much?"

"Am I?" He continued to laugh at my expense. "Tell you what, it's twenty minutes to breakfast, so I'll answer what you want to know, but for every question I answer, I get one answered, too."

I chewed on my hangnail. I knew Killian would want answers to the hard questions, and I wasn't sure I was ready to share that much with him. In the end, I wanted answers more than I wanted to keep secrets.

"Why psychology?"

He tilted his head and pursed his lips. "The girls have been talking." He pulled out of the ranch and onto the highway. "I like looking into people's minds, why they behave like they do, what triggers responses, that kind of thing."

"I must be fascinating to you."

I hadn't considered that I'd be a project for Killian, but why not? There was no other reason for him to want to hang out with me except maybe his loyalty to Mickey, Holly, and his brothers.

"You are, but not for the reasons you think. I'm not looking for a project, Megan. I could find that in any bar in town. I'm just trying to be—"

"Neighborly, I know. You already said so."

I don't know why it irritated me so much, but hearing Killian say he was being neighborly rubbed me wrong. I'd run to my neighbor the night my mom accused me of seducing her latest man. She wouldn't listen when I tried to tell her he climbed into my bed. She kicked me out that night, and with nowhere to go, I went next door. Tyler took what I wouldn't give the stranger, but I supposed it was better to submit to the enemy I knew than to the monster I didn't. That was my life for the next two years.

"What's wrong, Megan?"

"Let's just say I didn't have a very nice neighbor, so when you say you're being neighborly, all sorts of unpleasant memories come to the surface."

Killian's knuckles turned white against the black leather grip of his steering wheel. "What did he do to you?"

"We don't have that much time. The better question would be, what *didn't* he do to me?" I turned and stared out the window. Life rushed past us at seventy-five miles an hour. "What was your childhood like?"

"That's an excellent question, and it will also answer the first one you asked."

Killian proceeded to tell me about his childhood. How as the youngest son, he was picked on by everyone, and when he wasn't being bullied, he was being ignored. He acted out a lot and found himself bent over a wooden horse, taking his belt licks from his father. He spent a lot of his time in the stables with the horses, and when his father threatened to send a disobedient horse to slaughter, Killian bartered what he had.

"So you traded good behavior for a horse?"

"No, I traded acceptable behavior for a horse. I'm no saint." He flipped on his blinker and turned into the parking lot of a diner called Trudy's. He killed the engine and finished his thought. "It was about that time I figured out I had control of my destiny, and often those around me. I liked the power of turning a misunderstood animal into a confident member of the herd. I learned so much about my ability to control myself. The horse I rescued was Dante, and he's one of the finest horses around. I'll introduce you to him later. We'll take him for a ride."

He hopped out of the truck and walked around to open my door. The last time a man opened my door, he was holding my head and putting me in the back seat of a cop car.

Chapter 9

MEGAN

After breakfast, we drove straight to the supply store. It was so much more interesting than a regular department store. They had everything from feed to clothing. While Killian picked out equipment for Lucky, I walked the aisles. He found me at the hats.

"Here, this one will look great on you." He pulled a white straw Stetson from the rack and popped it onto my head. It was so big, it covered most of my eyes. "How about this one?" He pulled a smaller size from the rack and adjusted it to my head. "Perfect. We'll take it."

"What?" I had no money for hats. "No."

"I insist." He pulled the hat from my head and slipped it under his arm. His eyes trailed down my body to my tennis shoes. "You need boots, too. Especially if I'm going to teach you to ride." He turned and walked away, forcing me to run after him.

"Killian, I can't afford boots, and I can't afford to owe you—"

"Stop. I'm not expecting anything in return. I'm just being neigh… nice. Isn't it time someone was nice to you without expectations? I'm also being selfish. Once you get proficient in the saddle, you can help me exercise the horses." He pulled a pair of brown boots from the shelf.

"How did you know my size?" I took the size seven boots he offered and sat down on the nearby bench to try them on.

"I'm observant. There is very little I miss. Let's try these on."

He showed me how to pull them on and explained how the heel was important in the stirrup, and why my tennis shoes would never work. By the time we left, he had me feeling like I was doing him a favor by letting him buy me ranch wear.

"I'll pay you back."

I looked down at the new boots I walked out with. Killian said within a few hours they'd mold to my feet and the heel wouldn't slip. They'd feel like a second skin.

"Megan, you're helping at the ranch, and if one of my other hands were lacking, I'd outfit them properly." He reached in the bag between us and pulled out a pair of pink leather gloves. "These are for you, too. I want your hands to stay soft."

"Pink?"

"Now you'll know exactly which pair is yours."

I picked up the gloves and held them to my nose. I loved the smell of leather. In the past few days, I had begun to associate it with Killian and the safety of the ranch.

The sun was high in the sky when we drove under the Second Chance Ranch sign. Colorado weather was unpredictable, and though yesterday was in the low double digits, today the heat melted the snow and warmed the plains.

I silently prayed Killian would get overheated and take off his shirt. No view was more impressive than the peaks and valleys of his muscled chest. Even the sight of the Rocky Mountains in the distance paled in comparison.

"Meet me in the staff stables in ten minutes. No is not an option."

I squared my shoulders. "Are you always going to boss me around?"

"Probably, but you have a voice. Care to use it?" He lifted his eyes and waited for my response.

"But you said no wasn't an option."

"And if you had an option, would you choose differently?" He pushed his Stetson back on his head.

Oh my goodness, he's been waiting for me to sound off. I've always had options. He just wanted me to realize it.

"Killian, from now on, I'd like you to ask me instead of boss me." I pulled my new Stetson out of the bag and pressed it firmly on my head. "I like your voice. Let me hear it." I tossed his words back at him. I'd never been so bold, but instantly I felt more confident. Was it the hat? Killian?

Bent over, he snatched a piece of hay from the ground and slipped it between his lips. Behind the hint of a smile, he said, "Megan, would you like to meet my horse? He needs exercise, and I'd love for you to join me."

I felt giddy. I knew Killian was just being ni…neighborly, but it felt so good to be asked something without feeling like there would be a toll to pay later.

"Yes, I'd love to meet your horse."

I turned in my new boots and made my way to my cabin. I needed to freshen up, and I wanted to take a look at this girl who was taking her first steps into a new future in a pair of cowboy boots and a Stetson.

Minutes later, I was in the staff stables watching Killian saddle his horse. Dante was a beast of an animal, big like his owner. He was intimidating as hell until he flipped my hat off my head.

"Hey." I bent over to pick up my hat, and Dante nudged my bottom, forcing me to fall forward. "What the heck?"

"He's just playing. He used to kick and bite, but he's learned acceptable behavior, and he's gauging your reaction."

I brushed my hands on my jeans and approached the horse from his left like Killian had shown me. After I ran my fingers through his mane, he reciprocated by running his muzzle through my hair until he sneezed and left the ends damp.

"Gross."

"To a horse, that's foreplay." Killian slipped something into the saddlebag and patted it closed. "Ready?"

Before I could answer, he'd lifted me to Dante's back and swung his body behind me. I was pressed between the saddle horn and a hard body. I scooted back, preferring the feel of Killian's body.

With a shake of the reins and a soft clucking sound from Killian, Dante moved to the gate like he'd done this a thousand times.

"Will carrying two riders hurt his back?"

"No, Dante is bull-strong. He's made of sturdy stuff." Killian wrapped his arms around me and showed me the proper way to steer a horse. "Just coax him. He doesn't need a firm hand anymore. Pleasing me is important because pleasing me comes with rewards."

He whispered the words in my ear, and I got the impression he was talking about more than his horse. We rode for the greater part of an hour and came to a crest that overlooked the ranch. In the distance, the Rocky Mountains rose from the ground. The sun cast glorious shadows across their white peaks.

"Beautiful. I may never leave this place."

Killian climbed off the horse and offered me his hand. I slid into his arms and down his body. He stopped my descent when our lips were lined up. I waited for the kiss, but it never came. He stalled, then allowed me to slide to the solid ground.

He reached into the saddlebag and pulled out a can of Sprite for me and a Coke for himself. I gave him a how-did-you-know look.

"I told you, I'm observant."

He laced his fingers through mine and walked me to the ledge, where we sat and drank the cold sodas in silence. I didn't need words to fill the space when so many words filled my head.

I broke the silence with a question. "Sunset didn't eat yesterday. When I cleaned her stall, her haynet was still full."

"I know you're worried about her, but there isn't anything we can do but comfort her and hope nature has the right plan." There was a hint of sadness in his voice. "This is her first pregnancy. She's young, only three, and if she loses this foal, we'll try again in the future. I'll give her another year or two to mature."

"Sad."

Did she know what was happening like I had known? I had seen the blood spreading across my pants, and I'd known I had one chance to save my baby. I'd taken it and failed. Poor Sunset had no options.

"Let's head back. Lucky is getting his first taste of Kill Camp." He stood and helped me to my feet. "I like this hat on you. Very sexy." He straightened my Stetson and whistled. Dante sauntered over like he'd been beckoned.

"Kill Camp?" It sounded painful.

"Short for Killian Camp. He's going to come out and play today. We're going to get to know each other a bit. Maybe even gain a bit of respect for one another."

When we got back, Killian showed me how to remove the saddle and brush down the horse to remove the salt from his sweaty coat. Once Dante was back in his stall, Killian left to get Lucky and I went home. I smelled of hay, horse shit, and Killian. Since I couldn't get rid of one smell and save another, I opted to wash them all away.

I pulled on clean jeans, a pink cotton tee, and socks, and slid into my new boots. Killian was right; they fit like a second skin.

The paper on the coffee table called to me, I sat down and wrote a few more things I knew for sure.

I love the horses.

I don't mind hard work.

Killian is too sexy for my own good.

With Killian in the forefront of my thoughts, I pulled my coat off the hook by the door and drifted toward the arena like a fish to a baited hook. Not wanting to interrupt, I took a seat on the bleachers to the right and sat quietly, watching.

To my untrained eye, it looked like Killian and Lucky were having a deep conversation. Killian stood at a distance, and after several minutes of inching forward, he stood next to the horse, his body off to the left. I would have given anything to hear what he said.

Seconds later, he repeated his actions. He talked, approached, and stood next to the horse. After several repetitions, Killian changed it up. He talked and took a step back. The horse took a step forward. Again and again, they repeated the exercise. Finally,

Killian talked and stood firm. The horse inched forward until he stood shoulder to shoulder with the big cowboy.

Killian's lips lifted into a broad smile. There was lots of praise, and Lucky was brought back to his stall. He must have pleased Killian because he was rewarded with an apple and a carrot.

I stood in the corner and watched Killian care for the horse. He cut the apple and carrot into pieces and tossed them into a bowl. "You don't have to hide in the corner. I won't bite…and if I do, you'll enjoy it." He never turned to look at me, but he knew I was there.

"I was just leaving. Feeling tired." I turned and walked away. I wasn't ready for another round of Killian.

Later that night, I snuck into the stables to visit Sunset.

Chapter 10

KILLIAN

She snuck into the stables like a thief in the night, but I saw her. I didn't choose the last cabin by accident; it gave me a panoramic view of the ranch. There wasn't much I missed. I'd been told I had uncanny sensing abilities, but the truth was, I manipulated my surroundings so they worked for me.

After a few minutes, I followed her, sliding into the opposite entrance. I kept to the darker side of the stables, not ready to make myself known. A thread of light illuminated her. Angelic but sexy, she stood in front of Sunset's stall. The horse peeked over the door and rubbed her muzzle against Megan's hair.

"I've been thinking about you a lot. How are you feeling?"

She reached up and combed through Sunset's mane. The horse nickered in response. Megan was a natural with animals. They liked her, and I'd trust animal instinct over human instinct any day.

"Are you scared?"

She leaned on the gate, her back to me. It was hard to hear what she was saying, but I picked up a few things, like her telling Sunset she was scared, too. Was she scared for Sunset, or was she referring to herself?

I'd never met a woman like Megan, brave on the outside, but

terrified on the inside. She needed the same care and consideration as Lucky.

My ears perked up when I heard my name. I slid into the darkest corner when she turned and walked to Lucky's stall. I almost popped out of my hiding place to tell her to back away when she got too close. Lucky wasn't a horse you trusted with abandon. He was a frightened caged animal, and those were the most dangerous types.

My boot was lifted and ready to move, but Megan stopped a foot or so from the front of his stall. I relaxed and leaned back into the wall.

"Hey, boy." Her voice was soft and sweet like a lullaby. "Can I tell you something?" She waited for a response from the animal, but if I were a betting man, Lucky had turned the other cheek and was giving her a backside view.

"Whoever did that to you was a coward. I don't know why men hit and maim or if they get some kind of thrill from your pain, but I hope you will heal, inside and out." She kicked at the hay beneath her feet. "I'm in the same boat as you, I've been hurt really bad, and I don't trust easily. I was lucky to go to prison. Imagine that... someone saying they felt lucky to go to prison, but I met Mickey, Holly, Natalie, and Robyn there, and now I'm here, just like you. You have Killian, and I hope he's as good for you as the girls were for me. See you tomorrow, Lucky."

She trailed her hand across the top rail of the stall and left. I stood in the dark and thought about what she'd said. She'd been hurt, she was trying to heal, and Lucky had me. Listening in on her private conversation was wrong, but I didn't feel guilty enough to stop. Megan hadn't divulged much. Shit, she had talked more to the horse than she did to me. That would have to change. I wanted her to know that she had me, too.

The next few days went the same. Megan and I would clean stalls, and she'd break around ten to talk to Mickey and Holly. I'd work with Lucky while she watched, and we would part for the night. She said she was studying for her driver's permit, but every night she'd sneak into the stables and stay for an hour or so. Sometimes I'd check in to see that she was okay, but I always stayed in the shadows. I never remained longer than a moment; something told me she had a lot to get off her chest, and if she had wanted me to hear her secrets, she would have shared them.

When it came to trust, I was making more progress with Lucky than with Megan. She was pleasant, but she was holding back. She still trembled, and her expression often looked like she was the prey of a wild animal.

"You ready?"

Today, she'd test for her permit. I didn't look forward to teaching her how to drive, but I was happy she needed me for something. After the trip to the DMV, she had a meeting with her parole officer. It was hard to believe Megan needed a PO, but I didn't know her whole story. She was held responsible for someone's death, and that should never be taken lightly. The problem was, I couldn't imagine her swatting a fly, let alone killing a man. She did say there were extenuating circumstances, and I intended to find out what that meant.

She chewed on her thumbnail. "I'm so nervous. What if I don't pass?"

"Then you take it again. You studied. You're smart. You'll do fine." We sat in my truck in front of the DMV for several long minutes. "Do I need to go in with you for moral support?"

"Can you pass me the answers?"

"No, you're on your own in there."

She looked at the door and back at me. "I guess I should brave it and get it done, then." With her shoulders pulled back, she opened the door and slid from the truck.

What compelled me to jump out of the truck and run to her side, I couldn't say. "Kiss for luck?"

I lowered my lips to hers and kissed her lightly. She stiffened at first, but when I wrapped my arm around her waist and pulled her against my body, she melted into the kiss. Maybe I was making more progress in the trust department than I'd thought. I didn't press too far. Sending her running wasn't my plan, but kissing her wasn't either.

She backed away and touched her lips. "Why did you do that?" Her tone was curious, not accusatory.

"I don't know. It seemed the right thing to do at the moment. Should I be apologizing?" I stepped forward, and she didn't retreat. "Say what you feel."

Her tongue slipped out to slicken her lips. The head in my pants began to twitch.

"Yes, you should be apologizing...for addling my brain."

"So you liked it?"

"Do you really need me to stroke your ego?" She stood tall, putting her brave persona in place.

"I like the idea of stroking." It was funny to watch her turn radish red. "Now get before I grab you and do it again."

She paused as if she was considering it, and when I shifted forward, she took off toward the door. That girl could move fast.

I sat in my truck for forty-five minutes, waiting for her to reappear. Why was her pull on me so strong? I had my choice of women, but I had a thing for the troubled ones. My father said I had a savior complex. I disagreed. If anything, I had an injustice complex.

She bounced out of the building, waving a piece of white paper in the air. Her smile was as bright as the snowcapped peaks of the mountains behind her.

I exited the truck and met her in the middle of the parking lot. "Oh, so you failed."

"What? No. I passed. This isn't the look of a woman who failed. I can see why you went into training horses; your ability to read people is awful." She stopped and put her hand over her mouth like she was trying to spoon the words back in.

"This calls for a celebration." I dangled the keys in front of her. "Do you want to drive?"

"Don't you think we should reserve the driving for after I have a lesson?"

"I'm insured."

"I'm not. I have to text Holly. She's going to put me on her plan."

"Fair enough." I opened the door and helped her in. "Off to your parole meeting, and then to Rick's to celebrate."

Rather than crush herself into the passenger door like she tended to do, she took up her side of the bench seat and relaxed, all the while staring at the piece of paper that said she could legally drive with me.

The women's shelter sat in the middle of downtown Denver. Flanked by a coffeeshop and dry cleaners, it looked more like a modern hotel than a safe haven for abused women.

"I'll wait here."

She paused before she opened the door. "Killian, I want you to know how much I've appreciated your friendship and support today."

"I thought you were opposed to stroking my ego," I hopped out of the truck and walked around to open her door. "Do you need another kiss for luck?"

Her lips twitched in a weak smile. "Get back in the car, cowboy. I'll be out in a bit."

It was good to hear her push back. A week ago, I never would have guessed she had it in her.

"I'll be here waiting for you to come back and stroke me again." Teasing her was becoming my guilty pleasure. Watching her grow as a person was the reward.

I stood in the middle of the parking lot and watched the sway of her hips until she pushed the bell to a secure door and was buzzed through.

I was in trouble when it came to Megan Connelly. Caring about her might have been requisite, but falling for her was foolish. I didn't do complicated. I didn't do long-term. I didn't do love, but I wanted to do her.

She walked out of the shelter thirty minutes later with a look on her face. It was neither happy nor sad, but somehow confused.

"Hey, thanks for waiting." She hopped into the truck and chewed on her thumbnail. "They offered me a deal."

"What do you mean, they offered you a deal?"

"I'm considered a low-risk parolee. If I volunteer one day a week at the shelter, I don't have to see my PO until my time is up in six months. Clocking in at the shelter counts as my check-in."

"That's awesome. How does that make you feel?"

"Not sure. I met the women staying here, and they remind me of me. I'm not sure I want to relive that one day a week."

I turned the key and drove toward Rick's. "It could be therapeutic for you. I don't know what happened to you. I hope to earn your trust so you'll tell me, but sometimes, facing your fears and beating them back can be good. Promise me you'll think about it."

She sank back into the seat and sighed. "I promise."

Chapter 11

MEGAN

We walked through Rick's Roost like salmon swimming upstream. Killian grabbed the last empty booth much to the disappointment of another couple reaching it at the same time. His steely glare sent them looking elsewhere.

"Stay here," he demanded before he left for the bar.

I obeyed, not because he demanded, but because there was so much to observe from my vantage point in the corner.

There were a lot of women and fewer men. The small stage where Ryker sang last week was empty, and no one was setting up. A jukebox in the corner played a country ballad. Neon bar signs lit the room. Today it smelled of wings and fries, or maybe that was the smell I'd associated with this place. Either way, my stomach grumbled. I'd eaten very little today because my nerves were on edge.

"Hope this is okay." Killian placed a mug of beer in front of me. "I also ordered food. They have the best burgers." He climbed into the booth next to me, our thighs touching, making it hard to inhale. "I know I should have asked first, but with as busy as this place gets, we'll be lucky to flag down anyone within the hour."

I picked up the beer and sipped at the foamy top. "Mmm, it's good."

He took a long drink. The foam stuck to the shadow on his upper lip until his tongue snuck out to wipe it free. "I love a cold beer after a long hard day."

I could sit and watch him drink beer all day. Sip. Foam. Tongue. Over and over again.

"What?"

He was laughing at me. "You make me smile. Your emotions show on your face like someone wrote them in black Sharpie."

"Really?" That didn't make me happy. All I was thinking right then was how much I wanted to kiss him again, and then I thought about how stupid I was behaving, but I'd test his theory. "What was I thinking?"

"Your eyes are still uncertain, but the wetting of your lips tells me you find me appetizing. Your body leans into me when you're not paying attention. I'd say you might want to kiss me again, but kiss me better this time."

I felt the flush rise on my face. "I'm hungry. That's why I licked my lips."

He turned in the booth, his knee grazing the top of my thigh. "Is that the lie you're telling yourself?"

"I'm not lying to myself."

"And another lie." He glanced over his shoulder. "You lie a lot to yourself, Megan." He shimmied out of the booth. "I'll be right back, and we can talk about it."

Dumbfounded, I stared into my beer and watched the bubbles rise to the top. Was he right? Did I lie to myself?

"I got us both bacon cheeseburgers. You got fries, I got onion rings. We'll share." Once again he was pressed up close to my body, and I wanted to say it bothered me, but that would have been a lie.

"I'm not accusing you of lying about the trivial things, although you do. I'm accusing you of lying to yourself about yourself."

I swallowed my bite of burger along with my agitation. "How so?"

"You try to convince yourself that men are bad, or at least bad for you."

"I...I...do." I tried to deny it, but I couldn't. Big men, little men, it didn't matter, I was afraid of them all. "I'm not afraid of you, even though I should be."

"You should be because I'm a man?"

"Yes."

"So…" He took a drink of his beer. "I have to pay for the sins of all men?"

He sounded just like Holly the day I left prison. "No, that wouldn't be fair, would it?" I played with one of my fries, trying to get the courage to ask the questions I wanted answered. "Have you ever hit a woman, Killian?"

"Define hit."

What is there to define? "Come on, Killian, let's not play games. Have you laid your hand to a woman's body?" I began to inch away, but Killian stopped my progress by laying his hand over my shoulder.

"Yes, I have, but she asked for it."

I broke free from his grip and slid into the curve of the booth. "No one asks for it, Killian." My voice cracked. "That's a lie *you* tell yourself."

He patted the booth next to him. "Come here, Megan." He waited and waited.

With a shake of my head, I said, "No," with more forcefulness than I expected to come from me.

He ran his hand through his hair. "Let me rephrase that for you." He popped an onion ring into his mouth. After what appeared to be contemplative thought, he spoke. "I've been with women who like to be…look, there's no easy way to explain this. I've tied women up, I've spanked them, and I've even choked a girl once because she needed it, not because I needed it. Like everyone, I've experimented in the bedroom and found there is a fine line between pain and pleasure."

"There's no pleasure in pain. Let me tell you, I've endured enough pain to last a lifetime. I'm waiting for life to bless me with pleasure." I pushed my half-eaten burger to the side, my appetite gone.

"Come here." He patted the vinyl next to him.

I looked from him to his hand on the seat. I wanted to crawl up next to him and forget about the conversation, but hadn't I been given enough passes in this lifetime?

"What about the whips in your living room?"

His eyes widened. "You've been snooping."

"No…yes. Holly said I should take a look in your living room before I started to fall for you." Half a beer, and my filter vanished.

"I'll tell you the story of those whips later, but I will guarantee you now those whips have never hit anyone or anything when in my hand."

Just as I considered sliding over to sit beside Killian, the willowy blonde from the other night plopped herself onto his lap and wrapped her arms around his neck. A wave of jealousy washed over me.

"Trish." Killian's voice was stern and unwavering. "Get the hell off my lap." He grabbed her waist and attempted to shift her out of the booth. She hung on like she was riding a bull and needed to reach eight seconds to get her prize.

"Oh, stop it. You know you miss me." Trish glanced at me, her only acknowledgment of my presence.

"Trish, I'm going to ask nicely one more time, and then I'll remove you myself, and you won't like it."

"Spanking girl?" I blurted. Shit, the damn beer was messing with me.

They both ignored me, although I did see the quick lift of an eyebrow from Killian and an almost smile.

"I'm out with Megan, Trish; now get the hell away from me."

He forced the issue by sliding out of the booth with her on his lap. He didn't let her slide down his body as he had me. He let her thunk to her feet, then sat back in the booth and patted the seat next to him.

"You never took me out. You only took me to —"

He cut her off. "Trish, I'm losing my patience." He looked toward the bar. "Go ride a different cowboy. I see Ron at the bar, I'm sure he'd be happy to make you behave."

I watched in fascination. Trish's face fell into a pout. Killian turned away from her and stared at me like she didn't exist.

"So, where were we?"

Trish took the hint and stomped away in her bedazzled purple boots and black miniskirt. Two minutes later, she was wrapped around another man's waist.

"I hope you get tested often. That girl is a walking petri dish."

"No glove, no love, baby." He reached for my hand and pulled me gently to him. "I think we were talking about you snooping."

"Guilty."

"And how maybe you're falling for me."

I pulled my thumb to my teeth and nibbled at the tender skin. "Maybe."

It happened so quickly; I didn't know how to respond. One minute I was sitting in the booth; the next I was sitting on Killian's lap and his lips were on mine. His kiss was as demanding as his questions.

"Kiss me, Megan. Don't be afraid, I'll never hurt you."

His tongue probed at my lips, seeking entrance. When our tongues touched, the room was silenced. If I'd been asked later, I would have sworn we were the only two people in the bar.

His hands ran up and down my spine until they came to rest on my hips. When he broke the kiss, I was drunk, but it had nothing to do with the beer. I'd never been kissed with such passion.

"Let's go home, darlin'."

He tossed some bills on the table, and we were on our way. When he called me over to his side of the truck, I didn't hesitate to move closer to him. I leaned my head on his shoulder and sighed. This was what a date was supposed to feel like.

"Happy." Killian was used to my one-word explosions. I'd been letting them free since he gave me the courage to use my voice.

"Me, too." The rest of the trip was spent in blissful silence.

In front of my cabin, I hemmed and hawed, trying to get the courage to invite him in.

"Do you want to come in?"

I'd never invited anyone into my home before. When I was

living with my mom, it would have been embarrassing. The house was always a disaster. I'd clean it at night when she was asleep, and by the time I got home from school, it was trashed. At Tyler's, I would have been beaten had I invited anyone in. His jealousy had no boundaries. He caught me outside talking to the mailman once, and as soon as the mail carrier turned the corner, Tyler dragged me by the hair into the house. It was the first time he'd ever seriously beaten me. After that, I never answered the door and rarely left the house. The risk was higher than the reward.

"I appreciate the invite, but you're not ready for me to come in, and honestly, I'm not sure I'm ready to come in." In front of my cabin, he kissed me until my knees grew weak, then he spun me around and patted me on the ass. To my surprise, I liked it.

When the door closed, I leaned against it like a teenager back from her first date. In truth, it was my first date. I went from meeting boys after school in the library to living with the devil. The in-between felt nice.

I rushed over to the paper on the table and wrote more of my facts.

I lie.

Killian's kisses evaporate my brain cells.

I'm happy.

I'd filled out so much about myself, and yet I still didn't know much about me. My nightly therapy sessions with Sunset and Lucky were helping free me from some of the anxiety I felt and putting to rest some of my hurts.

When it was dark and I was certain the stables were empty, I left my cabin. The last thing I wanted was to run into one of the hands when I was alone.

Sunset had gotten used to my late-night visits and often hung her head over the stall and watched for me. Or maybe that was the lie I told myself. Either way, she wasn't leaning over the stall, and she wasn't visible. I knew immediately something was wrong. I peeked over the edge, and she was lying on her side. The sounds coming from her were wretched. It was obvious she was in pain.

"Hold on, Sunset; I'll get Killian." I ran straight to his cabin.

Chapter 12

KILLIAN

I was stepping out of the shower when I heard the pounding at my door. It wasn't a soft knock, but a frantic call for help. When I heard Megan's voice calling my name, I raced to the door in only a towel.

"You need to come. It's Sunset. She's on the ground, and she's making terrible sounds."

"Shit." I tossed my phone to Megan. "Call Roland and tell him Sunset is losing her foal."

I ran down the hall, only to return seconds later pulling a shirt over my head. I grabbed my boots and pulled them over my sockless feet. I didn't have time to worry about comfort. Megan was on the phone talking to Roland when I ran past her on my way to the stables.

"Hey, sweetheart."

I entered Sunset's stall and kneeled by her head. Her breathing was labored, and sweat covered her coat. Every few minutes she would grunt, and on occasion she would screech. All I could do was calm her down and wait for Roland.

"Come here, Megan." I could feel her presence, even though I couldn't see her. She did something to me that made me hyper aware of her proximity. "Sunset likes you. Kneel over here and talk to her like you do every night."

Her eyes flashed wide, but she did exactly as I asked. "You know?"

"I see you come out to the stables. I'm glad you're talking to something."

I ran to the tack room and was back in seconds. After wrapping the horse's tail, I felt her stomach. I'd delivered my share of foals, but I waited for Roland. This was his specialty.

Headlights lit up the dim stables. Roland was gloved and on his knees in seconds. "Poor baby. Let's see how far we have to go." With his arm gloved to his shoulder, he lubed up and pushed his hand into the birth canal.

Megan cooed to Sunset while I turned up the lighting. "How's she doing?"

"She's not dilating, her contractions are weak, and she seems really stressed. It's going to be a long night."

Megan never stopped talking to the horse. She talked about growing up in downtown Denver. She talked about her favorite childhood memories of long afternoons spent in the public library. She loved pralines-and-cream ice cream, *Jeopardy*, and mocha lattes. She talked about her graduation and the scholarship she was offered but didn't go into details as to why she didn't accept it. She was smart and pretty, and damn it if I wasn't starting to think of her as mine.

"Megan, darlin', can you make coffee for Roland and me? I'd be forever grateful." I offered her my hand to help her stand.

"Forever grateful?" Despite the sorrow I knew she was feeling, there was the brave girl trying to tease.

"Yes." I walked her out of the stables and held her in my arms for a moment. "It's going to be okay." When she leaned back and looked at me like her life depended on the validity of my words, tears were filling her eyes. I didn't know what to do, so I did what I did best. I kissed her.

Moments later, she rubbed at her eyes. After a deep breath, she stood straight. "What do you want in your coffee?"

"Two sugars. I like it sweet like I like my women." I cupped her cheek, trying to convey emotions I wasn't ready to speak. "Roland takes his black." She nodded, turned, and left me staring after her.

Roland was giving Sunset an injection when I entered.

"That will help move her along." He checked on Sunset's breathing and heart rate, then leaned against the wall. "What's going on between you and Megan?"

"Nothing, really. She's nice. I'm keeping her busy while the girls are away. She got her permit today; care to give her driving lessons?"

Roland chuckled. "That's way outside my job description. Glad you're looking after her. She needs someone to help her forge a path forward. Just don't hurt her."

I sat next to Roland and rested my hands on my knees. "Why in the hell does everyone think I'm going to hurt her?"

"You're not a long-term guy. She needs someone who will be there through thick and thin. Someone who will prove not all men are shits."

"You got all that from one lunch with her? She tells me nothing. I learned more tonight while she was chatting with the horse." I lowered my head to my hands and rubbed at the fatigue that had set in my jaw.

"She had nothing to lose by being open with me. She likes you in a different way. She has more on the line."

Megan appeared with two mugs of steaming coffee. "Here you go." She handed me a blue mug. "Sweet for you because that's how you like your women." She stepped over me and offered Roland his mug. "Yours is black like you like your… " We both looked at her in anticipation. "Your…coffee."

The next few hours went the same as the first. Lots of grunts and occasional high-pitched screeches, and sounds of Megan's soothing voice calming Sunset down with each contraction.

Finally, Roland called out, "Here we go." A portion of the red bag slipped from Sunset. Roland was up to his elbow. Within minutes, a foal no bigger than a kitten was delivered and Sunset was struggling to get back on her feet.

Roland and I were so intent on making sure Sunset was okay, I didn't notice Megan until I saw her sitting in the corner with the dead foal in her arms. Tears ran like a river down her face. She had her shirt wrapped around the fetus like she was cradling a baby. I knew she'd be sad, but I had no idea of the level of devastation she would experience.

"Darlin'." I kneeled in front of her and tried to remove the fetus, but she held it tight to her chest. She was soaked through and shivering. "Megan." I lifted her chin to look at me. "Roland needs to take the foal." She looked at me like I was asking her to give up her own child.

She slowly unfurled her arms and allowed me to take the bundle. "I couldn't save mine either." Her head fell to her knees, and she sobbed uncontrollably.

What the hell? I handed the foal off to Roland. He could see to Sunset; I needed to see to Megan.

She was light in my arms as I kicked open my door and carried her inside my cabin. Her teeth chattered, and her body shuddered. I'd had a different vision of undressing her for the first time. Putting her in a hot shower would have to do for now.

After setting her on the closed toilet seat, I turned on the water and waited for it to heat up. She sat still, and I wondered whether she was in shock.

"Megan, I'm going to undress you, but I need you to know it's only because you're wet and I'm afraid you're going to get sick or something." My words came out in a rush, very unlike the control I liked to wield in my life. I was scared to death. I had no experience with women who appeared to be catatonic.

I had her stripped down to nothing in seconds and standing under the flow of hot water. I stayed fully clothed, minus my boots.

She fell against my chest and sobbed. It was when I turned her around and moved her hair to the side that I let out the first words, "Motherfucker. Who did this to you?" Her left shoulder was scarred beyond belief. Puckers of skin the size of pennies marred her perfect body. Below them, two jagged silver streaks slashed across her back.

Fury filled me. There was no way these were accidental. They were too perfect in size to be anything but a cigarette or cigar burn.

Despite the heated water pouring over us, she shivered. "Let's get you dried and warm." I turned off the faucet and covered her body with a towel. "Stay here."

I rushed to my closet in my dripping clothes and pulled a T-shirt from the hanger. There was no doubt in my mind it would drop past her knees. Once I got her dry and clothed, I tucked her into my bed. There was no way I was letting her out of my sight. She lay balled up under my comforter, her expression blank. I was out of my wet clothes and into sweatpants and a clean T-shirt in seconds.

Snuggled up close, I rolled her against my chest and rubbed my hands down her body. It took at least ten minutes for her to stop shaking.

"I'm sorry," she whispered.

I slid my arms to her back and rubbed the scar tissue through her shirt. "No apologies necessary. Talk to me, Megan. What did you mean when you said you couldn't save yours either?"

Chapter 13

MEGAN

Dressed in nothing but Killian's T-shirt, I burrowed into his warm body and told him about my biggest failure. "I couldn't protect my child."

I clung to him like he was a raft on a raging river and plunged into the depths of my despair.

"Tyler's house was supposed to be a safe place to land." The sobs caught in my throat, but I choked them down. "Early on, he never hit me. He just took what he wanted in exchange for a safe place to stay. Then something changed." The long jagged breath I drew in propelled me forward. "He got paranoid and jealous. I couldn't look at anyone or talk to anyone. His anger went from yelling, to slapping, to beating me within an inch of my life."

"Go on." Killian's voice was tight and strained.

"I ended up pregnant because I couldn't leave the house to go to the clinic for my free birth control pills. Every time I left, he thought I was meeting someone. I paid the price for his jealousy. My safe haven became a prison." I ran my hand over my flat stomach. "I hid my pregnancy until I couldn't anymore. Tyler yelled at me for getting fat, but I knew deep in my soul he'd be furious if he found out. He'd never share me with anyone."

"Asshole," Killian grumbled.

"Definitely…anyway. One day, he caught me looking at my stomach in the mirror. I wasn't showing much, but a baby bump was developing. The rest is history."

"I need to know, Megan. I need to know what he did to you." He pleaded with me.

I went to that place where I talked about the situation as if it were a movie I'd just seen. That way, it didn't feel like it had happened to me. It felt like it had happened to someone else, and their story was easier to tell.

"He raged about how stupid I was, then he yelled about the expense of having a child, then he beat me to within an inch of my life. I lay curled on the floor, protecting my baby while he kicked me with his steel-toed work boots." I closed my eyes and remembered the feel of the first rib that cracked. "When he began breaking bones, I moved my hands from my tummy, trying to protect my ribs, and he kicked me repeatedly in the stomach. I felt a gush of wet heat between my legs, and fear clawed up my spine."

"I'm sorry." He gripped me so tight, I could hardly breathe.

"It's not your fault."

"No, but I can understand why you distrust men so much. So, I'm apologizing for every man that did you wrong."

Here was a man who earlier told me not to hold him responsible for other men's shortcomings, and now he was apologizing for the entire species. "To end the story, I knew the only chance to save me and the baby was to run. I'd tried several times before without luck. He'd always find me and drag me back." A profound sadness grew in my chest as heavy as a boulder. I fought the tears that threatened to burst like water from a broken dam. "Anyway…the keys were on the counter. I ran for them and got to the car, but he was on my tail with his work truck." I closed my eyes and saw the metal, the dust, and the blood. "That's how I ended up killing him. I ran. He chased. We crashed. And my baby died."

Killian was on his knees, pulling back the covers. "Losing your child was not your fault, Megan. He took your child with callous disregard for your health and safety. It wasn't your doing any more than it was Sunset's that she lost her foal. It was out of your hands." His eyes followed my body from head to toe. "If I had been your man, I would have worshiped you from your head to your pink toes." He peppered my body with kisses. "If you were carrying my child, I would have come home every day with pralines-and-cream ice cream and rejoiced with every pound you gained. I would have been on my knees in front of you, kissing your stomach and thanking the heavens that I had you and our child." He pressed his lips to my tummy and kissed it before he rested his head on me.

I pulled him up my body and looked into eyes full of passion and regret. "Killian, you don't have to mend the woes of the world. I'll be okay. Hell, my therapist has been waiting for me to break for years, I'm sorry it had to be with you." I smoothed the creases of his frown with my fingertips. "Sunset's baby was tiny, pale, and lifeless. Holding that dead baby just triggered something inside me. Her loss felt like mine. It was like a hammer to my chest."

"Don't tell me you know what that feels like. If that bastard weren't dead, I'd kill him myself."

I flashed a quick smile. "No, I've never been hit with a hammer." Killian was usually pretty tight about his emotions, but I saw for the first time what relief looked like.

"This wasn't how I imagined spending our first night together." He rolled me over and pulled my back to his chest. "I had such a different vision of how it would go down, and the only thing that resembles my fantasies is you in my T-shirt without a stitch of clothing beneath." He wrapped his arm around my stomach and kissed the back of my head. "Goodnight, sweetheart. I'm so glad you're here, Megan."

"Wait. I want to hear the fantasy." I twisted in his arms, but he held me tight.

Killian laughed. "Not tonight. I'm holding it together by a fiber as it is. Go to sleep before I get other ideas."

Sleep seduced me with visions of Killian soaking wet in the shower. I woke to an empty, cold bed. For the first time in six years, I'd slept soundly. There was no fear, no nightmares, only dreams of a sexy man. His eyes were cornflower blue, his body carved from granite, and his voice low and sexy, telling me how happy he was I was here.

I lifted his shirt to my nose and inhaled his citrus scent. The clock on the table showed it was after eight. A tented note with my name sat on his pillow. My name written in his precise script caused my heart to flutter.

Megan,

Good morning, sweetheart. I hope you slept well. Stay in bed and rest, you had a rough night. When you're ready, your clothes are clean and at the end of the bed. The coffee is made, and I saved you a blueberry muffin. Sunset is doing well, but I'm sure she would love a visit from you.

Killian

I bounced out of bed at the thought of Sunset. Without Killian's warm body next to me, there was no reason to linger. After a quick shower, I threw on my clothes, grabbed the muffin and coffee, and ran straight to the stables. I wasn't sure whether I was more excited to see Killian or Sunset. When I arrived, they were both gone.

Panic set in until Cole told me they were both outside. I raced to the fenced-in enclosure and stopped dead at the sight of Killian bathing Sunset. His hands skimmed her body in the same fashion they did mine last night—soft and reassuring, without a question about their strength or intent. I leaned against the wood rail, mesmerized by the connection he had with his animals.

"Come on over. I'll show you how to groom her."

His eyes slid from the horse to me, and I knew immediately why the animals loved him. They trusted him, just like I did. Killian had me in a vulnerable position last night, and he took nothing from me. I wasn't sure how that made me feel. Out of all the men I'd ever met, Killian was the one I would have given myself to without reservation.

"How did you know I was here?"

"I can feel you."

I knew what he meant. There was something in the air that sizzled when he entered a room and something that died when he left. He felt it, too. That admission pleased me.

I pulled myself up to climb over the rail, and a splinter as large

Set in Stone

as an oak tree got lodged in my finger. "Shit, shit, shit, shit." I hopped to the ground and bent over like I'd been shot. Cradling my finger in the opposite hand, I cried. The damn thing felt like I'd been skinned to the bone.

Killian was beside me instantly, my hand in his. "Let me see." He pulled my finger to his mouth and sucked on it. His tongue swiped over the hurt, the heat of it soothing the sting. His teeth began to nibble, and in seconds he spit something to the side. "There you go." He stepped back and let go of my hand. The splinter was gone.

My knees were weak, but not from pain. Killian was unleashing needs in me I wasn't accustomed to—yearnings and desire other women talked about but had been foreign to me until this cowboy walked into my life.

"Kiss me." The words were out of my mouth before I could stop them.

"Kiss you?"

I lowered my head. Embarrassment heated my cheeks. "Yes, I need you to kiss me."

"Oh, now it's a need." He stepped forward, inches from me.

I held my breath in anticipation and lifted my chin toward him. "Please," I whispered when he took too long.

The feel of his lips against my neck brought goosebumps to the surface, and a warm heat spread down my body. When he trailed his kiss to my lips, I opened for him without thought. His tongue tangled with mine. His hands rubbed over my back and came to rest on my ass, where he squeezed and caressed until we broke for air.

The look in his eyes was carnal, and it should have sent me running, but it didn't. I wanted more. I needed more.

Killian's baby blues stared for countless minutes until Sunset reminded us she wasn't finished. "It's after nine o'clock. I already told you, this is a working ranch, not a vacation getaway." He nibbled on my neck and rubbed his palm over my bottom.

"Oh, I see." I laid my head back and enjoyed the sensations. "We're back to Killian the tyrant. Too bad; I was really enjoying Killian the kitten."

He lifted his hand and smacked my ass. The sting startled me, but his gentle caress afterward had me leaning into him and humming.

"Lesson one, the line between pain and pleasure is fine. That wasn't abuse—that was foreplay. But I have work to do, and that will have to wait." He walked backward, shaking his head but smiling. "You're driving me crazy, Megan."

"Bad crazy like I should get out of your way and leave you be, or good crazy like I should stay?" I inched toward him and the horse.

"Get over here and help me rub her down. There's no place I'd rather you be than next to me. Get used to it."

"Is that lesson two?"

"No, lesson two will *come* later." There was a lot of emphasis on the word 'come'.

"Oh." When I got close enough, he tugged me in front of him and pressed my ass to his front. I could feel the hard ridge of his erection through his jeans. After I rubbed against him a few times, he let out a painful groan. I let out a joyful laugh. "Are you sure I should stay?"

"I'm starting to second-guess myself. With you around, I'm likely to get nothing accomplished." He took my hand and showed me how to use something that looked like a squeegee. After Sunset was finished, he let her loose to roam free.

"She looks good. I'd never know she just lost her…" It was too hard to finish the sentence, so I let it drift.

"She can't dwell on yesterday. Only today matters, this minute, this second. What about you, Megan? Are you finished with yesterdays?" He gripped my hips and picked me up. My legs wrapped naturally around his waist.

"I'm done with yesterdays. I'm in this minute—this second—with you, and I need so much more." I willed my heart to slow down. Everything was happening so fast. Too fast? Yes. No. Maybe.

"What do you need, darlin'?"

His hands gripped my bottom as he walked me toward the cabins. All I had to do was say stop, and I knew Killian would put me down without a fuss. After all the years I'd screamed that word, stop wasn't in my vocabulary today. My body tingled with excitement in knowing that in minutes, this man would show me what passion felt like.

We rounded the corner and ran into Greer. He was tucking Trish into her car. They both stared at us with a look of contempt. Trish rolled her eyes. "Figures." She looked at me like I was the source of all of her woes. She got in her black sedan and revved the engine. The woman was an attention whore.

Greer looked at Trish as she backed out of the parking spot, then turned his attention back to Killian. "I don't mind leftovers." He adjusted his crotch. "See you tomorrow, Megan."

Before I could take my next breath, I was standing on the ground and Killian was beating Greer to a bloody mess. I heard the crunch of bone and watched as Greer crumpled to the ground with his hands covering his bloody nose.

"Pack up, asshole; you're out. I didn't fucking like you to begin with. You've got an hour to vacate, or I will pick your sorry ass up and kick it all the way off the property." Killian shook his hand and looked at his bloody knuckles.

Greer looked at me. "I just did you a fucking favor, Megan." He wiped the blood from his nose. "He packs a brutal punch."

Killian went after Greer again.

"Stop it. Just stop it," I yelled before I turned and ran to my cabin.

I had to get away. The blood, the sound, the yelling. It was all too much. I locked the door and curled into the tight space between the couch and the chair. The paper fell from the table and settled at my feet. I picked up the pen with a shaking hand and forced myself to write.

Killian has a temper.
His fists can do damage.
I'm stupid.

I didn't want to know any more. I scribbled across the notes, then crumpled the paper and threw it across the room. It hit the wall and rolled into the corner.

What the hell was I thinking? I'd let my guard down for the first man who was nice to me. Was he any different from Tyler? Fury boiled within Tyler on a regular basis, and when that anger got too hot to contain, someone always felt it. That someone was usually me. Was it the same with Killian? The next time he got angry and there wasn't a Greer to take it out on, would he come after me?

I ignored Killian's persistent knocking. If I had one look at his face, I knew I'd let him in. He'd proved himself to be violent and capable of inflicting pain, and yet he'd been kind, gentle, and loving. I buried my head against my knees and covered my ears with my hands. I'd never been more confused.

Chapter 14

KILLIAN

'Frustrated' was the only word that could describe my feelings at this point. I'd watched Greer stalk Megan repeatedly. His intentions were nothing but bad, and that's why I kept him fixing the fences even though I needed him in the stables. Keeping Megan close to me protected her.

Trish made the rounds with everyone, so seeing her with Greer wasn't a surprise. What drove me to violence were his words to Megan. She was no one's sloppy seconds; she was everything good and sweet, and damn it, I was falling for her.

She stayed in her cabin for the rest of the day. The next morning when I went to the stables, she had already started on the stalls. The horses were getting used to her, and she had listened well. She knew exactly which horses to put together, and which to keep apart.

She was at Lucky's stall, and I'd be damned if the horse wasn't nuzzling her neck like I'd done yesterday. Big, stubborn bastard wouldn't submit to me, but he was happy to move in on my girl.

My girl?

"I see you found a new admirer." She jumped at the sound of

my voice, and it nearly eviscerated me to see the fear back in her eyes.

"He seems happier than he was a week ago." She ran her hand up his muzzle and stepped away.

"He knows he's safe." I walked up to her slowly, like I did with a skittish horse. "You know you're safe, right?"

I lifted my hand to cup her cheek, but she turned away from my touch. A crushing pain squeezed my heart. I'd never been emotional over a girl, but Megan did something to me no other woman had. She made me feel.

"I only have a few more to go, and then I'll be out of your way." She picked up the rake and walked to the next stall.

"Megan, can we talk?" I leaned against Lucky's stall. He turned around, giving me his horse's ass view.

"There's not much to say, Killian." She picked up the half-full wheelbarrow and pushed toward the next stall.

"I disagree. I think there's a lot to say."

She put the wheelbarrow down and turned toward me. Gray shadows circled her eyes. Disappointment colored her face. Gone was the smile I loved, and in its place was the look of uncertainty.

"Not now, okay? I'm tired and confused."

I dropped my shoulders and nodded. "Let's go, Lucky."

I pulled the big horse out of his stall and led him into the arena. He picked up on my mood and decided to give me a hard time. His message was loud and clear. He was as unhappy with me as Megan was. I couldn't blame her. I'd scared the hell out of her. Her only experiences were with men who took from her and beat her. I would never be that man, and I'd prove it.

I worked with Lucky for several hours, casting glances over my shoulder in the vain hope she had snuck up on me. I felt her absence like a chunk had been dug from my chest.

It was useless to work with Lucky and his attitude when mine was just as bad. I pulled the lead from him and let him run the arena with Sunset. They were opposites but seemed to complement each other in mood and spirit, the same way Megan and I did.

I needed to get an attitude adjustment, and I knew just the girl who would give it to me.

When I reached Megan's cabin, she was sitting on the porch swing and talking on the phone.

"Yes, I know what you're saying, but I'm not sure I can believe you. I'm pretty good at reading people these days, and I never would have guessed he'd have that kind of temper. He's always buttoned up and in control." She looked up and saw me. Worry wrinkled her brow. "I have to go. Yes, I promise. See you guys in a few days."

The wind stopped, the birds quieted, and silence swirled around us. "Megan, I'm sorry. I was such a dick." Her heavy sigh worried me.

"Yes, you were." Her eyes closed, and her fingers rubbed at a snail's pace across her forehead. It was like she was trying to erase a memory.

At least she was back to trying on her brave demeanor. That was the girl who fought back and said what she felt. I could work with that. That girl showed up. The frightened Megan hid in her cabin and did God knows what.

"I'm sorry." I looked at the space beside her. "Can I sit down?"

She eyed me for a moment before she nodded. "I owe you an apology, too."

"You do?" I was baffled. What would this woman ever need to apologize to me for?

"I was talking to Mickey and Holly, and they reminded me that you were a good man and were protecting me."

At that moment, I wanted to find Holly and Mickey and hug them. "I could have handled it better."

"In the moment, I think you did exactly what you knew how to do, and I did the same. You fought, and I ran. We're quite a pair, aren't we?"

"Are we a pair?"

It was the scariest question I'd ever asked in my life. A lot was riding on it. Somehow, in my gut, I knew Megan was good for me. However, I wasn't sure whether I was good for her. Was she the one, or the one for now? I had a bad track record when it came to women, and I'd already fucked it up so bad. Was there a chance to redeem what we were building?

"There may be hope for us yet." She gripped my arm and leaned into my shoulder.

I needed her close. "Come here, Megan." When I lifted my arm, she slipped comfortably against my chest.

"Killian, I need something."

"Anything for you, darlin'." God, I was hoping she wanted me to carry her into the cabin and make love to her.

"Follow me." She rose off the porch swing and held out her hand.

My heart raced like a wild stallion. "Where are we going?"

"Your cabin. There are five whips hanging on your wall that need explaining." She pulled me off the swing and led me to my door.

When we entered, her eyes followed the whips in order. She walked to the black one and pulled it down from the hook. "Tell me about this one."

"This is going to take a while. Do you want a drink?"

I didn't wait for her response. Instead, I went to the refrigerator and pulled out two cans of soda. I had stocked up on Sprite for her and Coke for me.

She was running the tail of the whip through her hand when I approached. After covering her hand with mine, I took the whip and laid it on the coffee table. She took a seat while I remained standing.

"As you know, I have control issues. I try to control everything in my life. It helps me keep things in perspective. It also helps me protect the things that are important to me."

"What's important to you?" She shifted on the couch and pulled her knees to her chest. Classic defensive position. "Have you ever considered that to control the situation, you may be demanding something people can't give you?"

"Yes."

She pulled her knees tighter. "I'd never give you control. I hope you would never ask me to."

"I need to feel in control. I can't help myself any more than you can when you flinch and quake from fear. We all have survival mechanisms, and control is mine."

"You realize control is just a façade, right? You can't really control anything. There are too many variables."

"When did you become the psychology major?"

"I've gained a little insight after being in therapy for three years."

"Perhaps you're right." I sat on my haunches in front of her; the chain that hung from my belt loop clanged against the table. "I'll work on it. I'm gonna mess up because it's ingrained in me, but I'll try to be less controlling and more diplomatic."

She nodded and glanced past me to the whip on the table. "Now tell me about the whip."

I ran my fingers over the braided handle. "I have a thing for protecting the underdog. It doesn't matter if it's a horse, a dog, or a person who can't protect themselves, I'm drawn to them." Rocking back and forth gave me a rhythm for the story. "I was fourteen, but I was big for my age and I used my size, silence, and stubbornness to intimidate people. Being the youngest boy wasn't the easiest."

I rose up a few inches and sat on the table, never taking my eyes from her. "One day, my dad took me to a neighboring ranch. He'd heard the trainer had good results with his horses and wanted to see his technique. It didn't take long to figure out his technique. When I saw him slicing the whip through the air and hurting the stubborn stallion, I reacted. All the years of being picked on surfaced, and I took the whip from the trainer's hand."

I grabbed the black handle. "Let's just say I threatened to use the whip in the same manner it was used on the horse. Did I say I was big? Needless to say, I got my first paid job that day. The owner made me train his horses until he could find a replacement."

She slid her legs to the floor and laid her head in my lap. "I'm glad you were there. What happened to the horse?"

"I trained him, and the owner sold him. I split my time between the family ranch and Dawson's Ranch that summer. The other four whips have similar stories. They were taken from their owners to stop some form of abuse, and I keep them as a reminder to always protect the underdog."

"What about the chain?" She ran her hand over the silver links. "I've seen you reach for it twice. Once to basically hog-tie that guy in the bar, and then you reached for it with Greer."

I pulled the chain free. It was a dog collar. "I've had it since I was a kid. It belonged to my yellow Lab. When he died, I carried it with me to remind me of loyalty. It's turned out to be quite handy. You never know when you'll need to catch a stray animal, stop an asshole from assaulting a woman in Rick's or tie open the barn doors."

She lifted her head and looked at me. Her velvet brown eyes were filled with understanding. Her acceptance was overwhelming. "You realize everyone around here thinks you're into kinky sex. Whips, bondage, stuff like that."

"I know." My grin couldn't be suppressed.

"You like that they think of you that way?"

"People will think what they want, and Trish and her fetish didn't help. Then there was last Halloween, when I carved cuffs and a whip into my pumpkin." I shrugged my shoulders. I had no excuse to offer.

"So you're not into bondage and spankings?"

"Oh, darlin', I'd love to tie you up and turn you over my knee and spank your ass."

"Why?" Her mouth dropped open, but she didn't retreat.

"Because the minute you relinquished complete control to me, I'd know you trusted me implicitly. Your trust is what I'm after, Megan, so your submission would be a gift. But I'd never demand it."

"What about your need for control? You want to control me, and I don't want to be controlled."

"It's more about my need to control myself than it would be about controlling you. I'm stubborn. I like what I like, and I want what I want."

"What do you want, Killian?"

I sat in silence and considered her question. What did I want, and to what end? I was out of my element with Megan. She unbalanced me. I'd always known exactly what I wanted, but I had a feeling a quick fuck would never be enough, and I wasn't sure I was ready for more. I'd lost control of this situation, and all I could tell her was the truth.

"I want you."

"I want you, too, Killian. More than you know, and more than I should."

I didn't waste another minute. She was in my arms, then in my bed before she could change her mind.

I stood back and stared at her. Face flushed from rapid breathing, she was beautiful. "Are you sure?" I didn't want to give her the option to say no, but she needed to understand I'd stop if it became too much. My goal was to make sure it was just enough. This had to be perfect because it would set the tone for days to come.

She nodded her head but didn't say the words.

"Megan, I need to hear the words." I pulled off my shirt, and her eyes ate me up.

"I'm sure, Killian; in fact, I've never been surer of anything."

That was all I needed. I undressed her slowly, making sure to worship every part of her body. I especially liked her black bra and panties.

"I like these." I pulled the lace at her hips and inched the sexy lingerie down her smooth legs.

"Holly thought someone would like them."

"No one else better like them." I tossed them to my dresser, fully intending to keep them for myself. The thought of another man seeing her didn't sit right with me. I never considered myself the jealous type; simply the protective type.

Her voice came out in breathy wisps of air. "Are you getting possessive?" Her eyes were heavy, and her lips glistened from the wet sweep of her tongue.

"Yes, I guess I am. Someone can ride my horse or ride my bike, but no one will ride you but me."

I kicked off my boots and climbed up beside her. The strain in my jeans was painful, but it reminded me that Megan had endured pain throughout her entire life. I could endure a little to make this moment perfect.

After minutes of kissing, her lips resembled ripe raspberries, then my exploration led me south. She shuddered when I hit that sensitive spot where her neck and collarbone connected. I nipped and kissed until she couldn't hold still. Next, I slid my tongue down the center of her chest until my face was buried between her perfect breasts. She smelled sweet like sugar cookies.

Her nipples hardened and poked through the lace of her bra. I removed the flimsy material and tossed it to the side. *God, she's beautiful.* I traced every inch of her with a heated gaze. The perfection of her porcelain skin, the rise of her full breasts, the tight rosy buds that begged for attention were chipping away at my control. All I wanted to do was rip off my jeans and sink myself inside of her. Instead, I spent a lifetime pulling those tight little buds into my mouth until she begged for release.

Control, control, I chanted silently inside my head, but every bit of restraint was lost when I slipped my hand between her legs and found her slick and ready for me.

Chapter 15

MEGAN

A riot of emotions and sensations flooded my body. Bolts of electricity surged through every place he touched. I ached and pulsed with a need I couldn't define. Every kiss made me want more. Every nip and tug had me crying out for relief. I didn't recognize myself: where had the woman who shook and hid in closets gone, and who was this woman taking her place? I should have always been this woman—a woman with value and potential, full of hope, love, and passion.

"Oh, holy hell," I cried out when he pressed his tongue against my throbbing center. It was too late to stop the fall. I tumbled over the edge in a full-bodied explosion. Pleasure seared through every cell.

"Fuck, I could spend my entire life right here."

He swirled his tongue and pulled every last shudder from me. When I lay limp and boneless, he removed his remaining clothes, rolled a condom onto his stallion-like length and crawled between my legs. I was too spent to worry about anything. All I could think about was connecting with this man in the most intimate way possible. I relaxed and gave in to his power.

"Are you ready?" He lined himself up, but he didn't press forward.

I lifted my hips, forcing the tip of him inside me. "I want this, Killian. Connect with me. I need this." I needed to feel something other than fear, guilt, and regret. I needed to get in touch with the happy girl I'd buried years ago.

He pressed into me inch by slow inch. His arms shook, his jaw clenched, and a bead of sweat glistened on his brow. Restraint was etched into his face. He went slow and let my body adjust. Once rooted, he growled—and for the first time in my entire life, I felt sexy.

"You okay?" His voice wavered.

"Killian, let's do this already." I pushed my hips into the mattress, forcing him to pull out, and then I raised them to meet his. That was all it took. Killian found a rhythm that drove me insane. I was on the edge again, and I begged him for release. He shifted his body, making sure to connect with the parts that would throw me off the edge again. This time I tumbled calling his name, and he fell with me. We were a twined mass of jangled nerves and sweaty bodies. Several minutes later, he pulled out of me and disposed of the condom.

When he pulled me into his arms and held me, I whispered, "Safe."

I woke up later to a tickle on my damaged shoulder. Killian was sitting cross-legged behind me with a pen in his hand. The man was drawing on me.

"Are you marking your territory?" I tried to turn, but he held me in place.

"No, but that's a good idea." He leaned over me and wrote his name on my left breast, then went back to work.

Giggles bubbled from within. "At least you didn't pee on me. Sometimes you're such a caveman."

"I'm happy to oblige if that turns you on, darlin'." He made a mock play for his pants.

"Don't you dare." I squirmed away from him and crawled from the bed. "What are you drawing on my back?"

I walked into the bathroom and looked over my shoulder. What I saw silenced me. Every burn mark had been turned into a daisy. The slashes sprouted grass and looked like land. Killian stood behind me, smiling.

"Oh. My. God. You turned ugly to pretty."

I stared at the ink. The way he'd layered the petals and colored in the centers to cover the deepest scars was impressive.

"Nothing about you is ugly." He pressed his lips to the top of my head.

"Killian, could this be a real tattoo?" I looked over my shoulder again and fell in love with what he'd done. "This was the last reminder of my past. You've erased everything else."

"Tattoos are forever, Megan."

"I thought scars were, too?"

What started out as a kiss landed us breathless and tangled once more before he shuffled me out of bed and into the truck. He wouldn't tell me where we were going, but I didn't care. I was with Killian, and I was happy.

He pulled up in front of a tattoo parlor called Ace's and killed the engine. "They do a great job. They did mine several months ago."

"I want it so bad, but I can't afford a tattoo. I'll have to save up and come back another time." I pasted on a hopeful smile, trying to hide my disappointment at having to wait.

"Nonsense, we're putting the past to rest today. You're no longer the Megan Connelly you were yesterday. You don't have to get a tattoo, but if you want one, then let's do it. I'm sure I can find a way for you to compensate me for my generosity." He reached over and pulled me in for a short kiss. "What's it going to be?"

I stared at the door to Ace's and back at Killian. The choice was mine, and it felt amazing. I pressed my lips to his and showed him how grateful I was.

"Let's go, cowboy. I can't believe I'm volunteering for pain." It was crazy, but this time the pain was my choice, and I welcomed it.

He hopped out of his truck and pulled me into his arms. "I'll make sure you have double the pleasure later. Friends take care of friends."

I walked into the building with one question lingering in my head: at what point did being friends become something more?

Several hours later, I was coated with goo and wrapped in plastic. The tattoo hurt like hell, especially on the scarred parts, but I was happy to feel it. It erased the years I'd been tortured. I vowed right then that I'd never discuss the past again.

I gravitated toward every mirror so I could look over my shoulder at my ink. Dark turned to light, grim turned to bright, and the feeling of happiness made me lightheaded.

That night, I lay naked next to Killian feeling like a beautiful woman without a past, only a future. We devoured each other like two people who hadn't been fed in ages and then fell asleep wrapped in each other's arms.

Around five-thirty in the morning, I woke to the tenderness of Killian's kiss as he left for the stables. The intersection of my two favorite parts of ranch life—the horses and Killian—made me smile through my fatigue.

I dragged my sore body from the bed and dressed. My shoulder was tender, but it couldn't compete with the ache in every muscle of my body. Killian's many hours of pleasuring me hurt so good.

The coffee was made, and on the counter sat a box of Lucky Charms. The man was trying to possess my heart as well as my body. I was well on my way to falling hard for him, but I wasn't sure where he stood. Were we friends, lovers, or something more? I had no point of reference, no experience to help guide me.

Tyson and Cole were in the stables when I got there. They were leading the horses out, emptying the stalls for cleaning.

"Hey, Megan."

Tyson was leading the miniature horse out to pasture. *His* name was Princess. No wonder he bit people—he'd been misrepresented since the beginning.

"Hey, Tyson. I'll work on the stalls if you want to see to the horses. Killian said something about grooming and exercise today."

"You're going to keep cleaning stalls?"

I laughed at his incredulous tone. "What? This is a working ranch." I pulled my pink gloves from the wall and grabbed the rake.

"You've been hanging out with Killian too much." He tugged the little horse and left me to do what I did best—muck things up.

I was bent over sprinkling bedding pellets across the floor when I felt large hands on my ass. Killian had an obsession with grabbing my bottom.

"You better stand up. I'm getting impure thoughts again."

I ignored him and wiggled in front of him. "Oh, shut up. Aren't you ever sated?"

He came up behind me and wrapped himself around me. "Oh, baby, it's time for lesson two."

"Lesson two?"

One minute, I was in a stall raking up piles of dung; the next, I was in the tack room laid out on a horse blanket, naked from the waist down. When his heated tongue pressed inside me, I lost myself in the moment. It didn't matter that Cole and Tyson were on the other side of the door. When I was with Killian, nothing else existed. He sucked me into a bubble where nothing else mattered.

He licked and laved until I pulsed under his lips. My calves cramped, my stomach hurt, and my throat felt raw from screaming his name.

"You like that?" Killian lifted up and watched me. His lips glistened with my arousal.

"I do. I love it." Oh, did I love it. It was new and powerful, and it made my body twitch in pure pleasure.

"Me, too. Lesson two, Megan: I'll never be sated. Not because you don't satisfy me, but because I can't get enough of your taste, your touch, or your body, and when your tight little package squeezes around me, I'm fucking lost."

Somewhere in the middle, he'd dropped his pants and gloved up. He centered himself over me and pushed inside. My hips rose to meet him, wanting more, needing everything. Braced on his strong arms, he hovered above me.

"Look at me, Megan. Watch our bodies connect," he commanded, his voice a possessive growl.

I rose on my elbows and watched him enter me completely. I was stretched wide around his girth, filled to capacity. My head fell back, no longer able to watch while he pressed himself deep inside me. I moaned with satisfaction. Somehow, this man had filled more than my body. He'd filled the hollow places in my heart.

"Megan." His voice was tight, barely restrained. My eyes snapped open and stared into his lust-filled gaze. "You're so perfect."

He pressed deep inside me and paused, his eyes closed, and his body shuddered. A look of pure bliss covered his face. We were surrounded by dirt, and leather, and the smell of manure, and it was flawless.

We didn't lie together long; there was too much to do, and it wasn't fair to leave Tyson and Cole with everything while we fucked with abandon in the tack room. I hadn't thought much of this room the last time I was here, but obviously it held more than a Band-Aid for me now.

Killian left first, to make sure Tyson and Cole weren't in the stables to embarrass me. When I walked out, he was leaning against the wall, looking tall, dark, and sexy. He'd hung up his Stetson, and his hair had that messy just-had-sex look you read about in books. Normally serious and stoic, Killian looked like a happy, younger version of himself. I loved this Killian, the one who didn't take things too seriously, but I also loved the tall, dark, and dangerous Killian, too. He made my blood hot and my panties wet.

"Hey, beautiful. You were saying you liked to be asked and not told, right?"

After being bossed around my whole life, I was ready for a change. "I'd like to give it a try."

"Would you care to join me for dinner? A real date." He pulled his hat from the hook and pushed it perfectly on his head.

"You're asking me on a date after we—" I looked toward the tack room.

"Had sex in the tack room?"

Killian and I had known each other a week, and in that week I'd fallen for him. I couldn't call it love yet, but I was on my way. Was it just sex to him? It was so much more to me. He had liberated me.

"You don't have to take me to dinner." I walked toward him like he was metal and I was a magnet. "I can cook for you."

His shirt hung open, exposing his beautiful tattoo. When I palmed his chest, he held my hand over his heart. The rhythm was strong and steady.

"Having you cook for me sounds amazing. I can see you in nothing but an apron, your perfect, bare ass hanging out in the back, leaning over the oven to check on the baked chicken." He pulled my hand to his mouth and kissed my knuckles. "As appetizing as that sounds, I still want to take you out. You're driving. I'm buying. We'll go to Tommy's; it's the place where Mickey started a bar fight on her first night out. Kerrick describes it as the night his life began. The night he fell in love with her."

Tha-thump, tha-thump, tha-thump. My heart galloped. "The first day he met her?"

"I guess it happens that way for some."

I pulled my thumb to my mouth and nibbled at nothing. I'd gnawed the hangnail off days ago; now it was just a nervous habit. I let my hand fall to my side and asked the question that had sprung to my mind.

"Have you ever been in love?"

He backed up and leaned against the wall. Mr. Cool and Calm was back. He crossed one foot over the other, his posture that of a man without a care in the world.

"Nope."

"That's it? 'Nope' is all I get?"

"Yep."

"Argh."

I picked up my pink gloves from the floor, where I'd dropped them on our way to the tack room. He was by my side and holding me in place by my shoulders. Years ago I would have fainted on the spot, waking up later burned or worse.

"What do you really want to know, Megan?"

The man had an uncanny way of reading my thoughts. Sure, I

wanted to know whether a woman had ever captured his heart, but I was most curious about Trish. What part had she played in his life? When she left, she'd looked wounded, like she'd had more invested in him than a quick lay.

"How long did you date Trish?"

He groaned—loudly. "Trish and I were never an exclusive thing. We used each other."

"Why did it end?"

"It never began."

"Oh lord, you don't know anything about women."

He nuzzled my neck, sending shivers to my pleasure points.

"I think I proved to you a few minutes ago that I know a lot about women."

"Don't be a dick." I slapped him in the chest with my gloves. "You can't have regular sex with a girl and expect her not to fall in love with you."

"Yes, I can. I do it all the time." The words were wrong as soon as they came out, and by the look on his face, he knew it. "Not with you, Megan. It's different with you."

"Sure it is."

I yanked the gloves onto my hands and raked at the bedding like it was on fire, and my job was to beat it back. I don't know what I expected. He gave me no indication that we were more than friends. Deep down, I knew we were friends with benefits. The problem was, I didn't expect the truth to hurt so much.

"Come on, Megan, I answered without thinking." Killian blocked the stall door, but I pushed past him and into the next stall.

"It's not a problem, Killian. I get it."

"You don't get anything."

"Oh, now I'm stupid?"

He pulled his hat off and ran his hand through his hair.

"I've got stuff to do. Can we talk about this at dinner? I'd still like to take you to dinner. Meet me at the truck at six." He turned and left.

I'd given him the same back-sided salute that Lucky did. I didn't see him walk away, but the air left the room when he did. He was larger than life, and he filled every space when he was present. On the flip side, when he left the room, it felt as empty as a donut box after church.

I'm so stupid.

My body had the needs of a grown woman, but my head was still stuck in the fantasies of a little girl dreaming about her prince.

I had to get my head out of the clouds. Killian was no prince. We were friends; nothing more. Where in the hell were my two fairy godmothers when I needed them?

I tossed the shovel into the wheelbarrow and moved on to the next stall.

Chapter 16

KILLIAN

Lucky and I came to an agreement that afternoon. He would remain Lucky if he stopped being so stubborn. I pushed him hard, and by five o'clock he was eating out of my hand. Tomorrow, I'd saddle him up and see where that took me. Hopefully, I wouldn't be spending a lot of time on my ass. I felt like I'd already had it kicked by Megan today.

The minute my mind wasn't busy, all thoughts went to her. She was young and lacked experience, but I loved that innocent quality about her. It was the one thing that asshole didn't manage to beat out of her.

She was also really good at turning my words around to make me look like an asshole. Did they teach that shit in school? Oh hell, who was I kidding? I *was* an asshole. I didn't need her to make me one. I had that down pat. It had worked for years, but I had a feeling my life was about to change.

When I rounded the corner, Megan was leaning against Cole's truck. They were laughing like old friends. My initial reaction was to hightail it over there and punish Cole for talking to her. My mind raced at the awful chores I could assign him. Sanding rails and fence checks were at the top of my list. One would keep him busy for months, and the other would keep him in the fields for days. Both served the purpose to remove him from Megan's presence, but that would be wrong. In the end, I gave them both a hard stare and walked away.

I'd known Cole for a while, and he never grazed in another man's pasture. The problem was, I wasn't sure Megan was mine. We'd talked about being friends, but she sure felt like more than a friend. It seemed clear-cut this afternoon when she came on my tongue, but now things seemed uncertain because I'd let my mouth open before my brain could veto the words.

We'd been together for a week. It was a long week. A hard week. A glorious week. But did I have a right to claim her? Did I want to? Hell, the woman had spent the past six years of her life a prisoner, and I was trying to do the same. If I was honest with myself, I wanted to hide her away and make her mine, but that was selfish and wrong.

Freshly showered, I waited outside by my truck. She stomped out of her cabin at exactly six o'clock. I dangled the keys in front of her, but she ignored the gesture and walked toward the passenger side.

"I said you were driving. Take the keys." My voice filled with frustration. This woman pushed all my buttons.

She rounded the truck and pulled them from my grasp. She didn't grace me with the big smile I loved, only the upward turn of the lips that bordered between sweetness and cunning serial killer.

"Get in the truck, cowboy." She hopped in the driver's side before I could respond.

I climbed into the passenger's side and buckled up. "Glad you decided to join me for dinner."

"A girl's gotta eat." She jammed the key into the ignition. "Just remember, I haven't driven in three years, and it didn't go well the last time. Now's your chance to back out." She revved the engine.

I pulled on the seatbelt, making sure it was fastened securely. "Let's hit it."

She put the truck in reverse and eased off the brake. I sat back and watched. Her stops were choppy, and her starts were worse, but she followed every rule to a T. No rolling through stop signs for her. Her blinker was on when it needed to be. She checked every angle before she changed lanes. She was the picture of control behind that wheel, and that bit of enlightenment unsettled me.

Tommy's was busy, but what could I expect? It was Saturday night, and people were letting loose. I found an empty table off to the side and handed Megan a menu.

"Megan, can we talk about earlier?" I needed to clear the air with her.

She ignored my question and led with her own. "Do you come here often?" She pulled the paper napkin from the roll of silverware and laid out the utensils like she was setting the table for a holiday meal.

"I come here or Rick's on the weekend to let off steam." The music was loud, and people were on a quick path to stumbling drunk. "It may be a while before the waitress gets here. I'll get us a drink. What do you want?"

"Sprite, please."

"You don't want a beer or wine?"

"I'm driving, and that would be irresponsible."

"I'll drive home. Enjoy yourself."

She appeared to weigh my offer and ultimately asked for a light beer. I was relieved. Megan after a beer would be so much easier to talk to than pissed-off, uptight Megan.

When I returned with her beer, she was gone. I scoured the bar and found her playing pool with several women. After looking at the group, I knew I was on a straight path to hell. Every woman at that table had been under me at some point. I'd had them all, but out of the lot of them, Megan was the only one I wanted to go back to again and again.

Fuck me.

"Got your beer." I lifted the mug and nodded toward our table across the room. I needed to get her away from them and fast.

"Thanks." She lifted up on her tiptoes and kissed my cheek. Was it a genuine kiss, or the kind of kiss a girl gave you just before she kicked you in the ball sack?

"I'm going to stay here for a bit. You go on and take a seat. Did you order us dinner, too?"

Alarms sounded throughout my system. What was the right answer? Yes, and then she'd tell me she wanted choices; or no, and she'd tell me she was starving and I wasn't thinking about her needs.

"I'll order now if you tell me what you want to eat." Behind her stood three women with their hands on their hips and frowns on their lips.

"You must be special—Killian is not the type of guy to give choices. His way or the highway, I'd say."

Carrie had been the first girl I'd hooked up with when I arrived in Colorado. She'd been fun for a while, and then one day she told me we'd make amazing babies. Talk about verbal castration; I never could get it up again with her.

"Hot dog with chips. Please."

She turned toward the women and ignored me. That was a new experience for me: it wasn't unusual for a horse to turn its back on me, but it rarely happened with women. I had no idea how to handle this situation, so I went back to my safe space. If I couldn't control the situation, I'd control how I approached it, and this called for observation and distance. I put the food order in and went back to the table, where I overanalyzed Megan's body language, demeanor, and facial expressions, or lack thereof.

She made her way to our table when she saw the waitress bring our food, but not before each of the women got a hug. Why did women have to hug each other like it was some kind of secret handshake to an exclusive club?

"Did you win?"

She climbed onto the stool across from me and pulled off the top part of the hot dog bun. After squirting on a line of mustard and ketchup, she capped it and brought it to her mouth.

My pig-headed man brain wished she were wrapping her lips around something else instead of that hot dog. I wanted to reach over and lick the dab of mustard caught in the corner of her lips, but she was too quick with the napkin.

"No, I lost, but I learned a lot."

This was where I was supposed to ask what she'd learned. No damn way was I being led down that path. The minute I opened that door, there would be no recovery and no closing that can of worms. I'd watched them all, and every once in a while every eye would turn to me. There was always one woman shooting red hot daggers my way.

"Well, at least you had fun."

"I'm not sure I could call it fun. It was enlightening." She bit aggressively into her hot dog. So hard that I felt my testicles rise in fear.

I wanted to know what the women had told her, but I wasn't a masochist. Instead, I made an attempt to convince her of how special she was to me.

"Megan, you're not like those women. It's different with you." Her eyes narrowed, and it was evident I was in more trouble than I originally considered.

She crossed her arms over her chest and leaned back.

"Yes, I am different from them, but those girls and I have so much in common."

Internally, I was screaming at myself because I'd talked myself into a corner. To get past this conversation, I'd have to ask a question that was better to avoid. Frustrated, I gave in.

"What could you possibly have in common with them?"

"Let's see." Big eye roll and a loud exhale. "I can recite a list." She leaned forward and began. "We all belong to a group referred to as the Kill Club. We've all had amazing sex with you. Everyone in the group fell in love with you and was summarily dumped."

"Not everyone. You and I are still figuring it out."

The room seemed to get smaller and warmer with each passing moment. All I wanted was to get Megan away from Tommy's and away from my mistakes.

"I already figured it out. Don't worry; it didn't take the three musketeers over there to educate me. You came with a warning label I didn't heed."

I reached for her. "I like you, Megan, and I want to see where this goes."

She pulled her hands from my reach and tucked them under the table. "This isn't going anywhere. I can't be the girl you pretend to love. That's just another form of control. I told you, I won't be controlled. I'm not upset at you; you promised me nothing, but your actions made me want more than you could give."

"How do you know what I can give?" My voice pitched like a boy hitting puberty.

She scanned the room and stopped at the three women playing pool. "History. The past is a great predictor of the future. Listen, we can still be friends."

My head spun. She was playing the fucking friend card again. "I'm not interested in being your friend, Megan." The words spilled out unchecked. "Shit, that's not what I meant." I white-knuckled the table. "I want us to be more."

Her lips puffed out with a long exhale. "This morning, I would have jumped at the chance to be more with you, but after tonight, I realize I need to be everything to me right now." She rolled her shoulders and twisted her neck like she was working something out of her system. "Can you take me home? I'm tired."

Chapter 17

MEGAN

How silly I was to think Killian and I had something going on that could last. Even the girls had warned me of his propensity to hit and run. He was no different from most men. It was his delivery that confused me. He didn't hide behind a calloused fist; he threw emotional punches that tore you up inside. He did the right things and said the right things, and when your heart was at its most vulnerable, he'd land the deathblow, the one that left you wondering why you weren't enough for him.

No, I didn't need that kind of emotional torture. The best move for me at this point would be to get my life in order without the influence or distraction of a man. Curled up in the corner of the couch, I pulled the *What Now?* book from the coffee table and opened it to the next section.

So intent on figuring myself out, I fell into the trap the book had laid out for me.

These are the lies you tell yourself, the second chapter read. The object of this exercise was to put a name to my fears. The pad of paper felt heavy in my hand. It was interesting how Killian had already called me on my lies—at least some of them.

I gripped the pen between my fingers and jotted down several lies I knew for sure.

The past is behind me. Even I knew my past would haunt me forever. Tyler's eyes hid behind my lids when I slept. His words haunted my dreams.

I have value. Of this, I was uncertain. At this point, I could shovel shit from horse stalls, but what else could I offer? Wasn't I always cleaning up the shit of my life?

It will be easy to get over Killian. That was the biggest lie of all, because in a matter of a week, I'd let him into me in every way possible. He'd infiltrated my body, my mind, and my heart, but I'd keep telling myself that lie if it made the hurt of not having him less painful.

Time for animal therapy. My jacket hung from the hook by the door. Below it lay the crinkled paper from my last exercise. I picked it up and shoved it into my jacket pocket, then walked outside.

It was dark, and the air had taken on the chill of an impending storm. The wind whistled a lonely ballad between the cabins. When I plodded past Killian's, my heart twitched. I could hear the sound of his TV, probably some sports program or an action adventure movie. I actually thought I knew him, but in reality I only knew the person he let me see.

It could have been my imagination, but I swore I caught the citrus smell of his skin on the wind. It took all I had in me to continue walking. I bartered with myself all the way to the stables. I could be that girl he slept with and nothing more, because those moments with Killian would be enough. The sex was that good. The world wasn't offering me life on a silver platter, but maybe I could enjoy the crumbs he would give me. Then I reprimanded myself for lying. I wanted more, needed more—I deserved more.

Sunset was leaning over the stall, as if waiting for me. She was one sweet girl. She'd taken her knocks and went forward with her life. I'd been wallowing in mine for years. There was a lot to be learned from the animal kingdom.

Never take yourself too seriously, you could be barbecued and on someone's plate by noon.

Never become superior, these animals could knock you flat on your ass in a second.

Accept those around you for what they are.

Don't make excuses for people, they are often exactly who they show you.

People, like animals, can change, but it takes patience and a leap of faith in the right person to gain that trust.

"Hey, girl." She loved it when I ran my fingers through her mane. It was almost as if she'd move her head to force me to scratch an itch or sooth an ache. I was used to her running her muzzle through my hair and inhaling my scent. It seemed to offer her comfort or pleasure. "How are you feeling?"

As if she understood my question, she whinnied, then exhaled a contented sigh. I'd pulled a carrot from the treat bin on my way in and broke it into smaller pieces. She took it gently from my open palm. Her gift to me was a handful of saliva.

Off to my right and down several stalls, Lucky tossed his head about. Was he jealous? I gave Sunset a pat and headed to the big brute of a horse.

"What's up, big man?" I kept my distance, but Lucky appeared to be reaching for me. I inched forward, making sure to keep my hands in my pockets. There was no way I was losing a finger tonight. When the girls came home tomorrow, I wanted to be intact at least physically.

Lucky and I did a kind of dance together. I pictured us in a waltz. I inched forward, and he inched back. I slid to the side, and he slid opposite, always mirroring my movements. Eventually, when I moved forward, he gave in and stood still. It wasn't the brightest idea for me to turn my back and lean against his stall, but I was tired and wanted to lean on something solid.

Before I knew it, Lucky had rested his head on top of mine. I supported his weight happily. It was a breakthrough with a horse that didn't trust anyone, and yet he was taking a chance on me.

"Are you happy here?" I asked. I slowly slid my hand up behind my head and stroked his neck. "I'm happy here, too."

The truth almost hurt. I was happy being here, even if I couldn't have Killian to myself. He'd given me so much in the short time I'd known him. He'd shown me what it felt like to make love—or at least to have amazing sex. Any previous orgasms I'd experienced were purely accidental, but with Killian nothing was accidental. He lived his life with intention.

"I don't know if I should be jealous of you or feel sorry for you." I pivoted around so I faced the horse. "Killian will be working with you every day, trying to earn your trust. He's going to push you and drive you crazy." Lucky lowered his head and pressed his muzzle against my face. "I don't think he sets out to hurt anyone. I think he's just trying to figure out his way in the world, like the rest of us." Without thought, I reached up and threaded my fingers through his midnight black mane.

Before leaving, I pressed my lips to the center of his forehead. Lucky didn't react. We had come to an understanding of sorts. I needed him to listen as much as he needed me to understand, and I did understand. Too bad we couldn't hide his scars with a pretty tattoo.

Noise at the door sent me jumping inches into the air. Lucky skittered backward into his stall. Out of the shadows walked Killian.

"How long have you been there?" Lord, I would die a thousand deaths if he'd heard my private conversations. I was happy to spill my guts to a stubborn gelding, but I wasn't ready to let Killian know how much he'd affected me.

The moonlight cast a shadow across his face, making it impossible to see his expression. *Everything is in the eyes*, he had told me, but damn it, his were leaving me in the dark.

"Long enough to see you make that big bully into a soft puddle of equine goo."

"Sorry, I didn't mean to get so close, but he seemed to need to be touched."

"We all need to be touched, Megan. I already miss your touch. Please don't stay mad at me." He leaned in and pulled me close.

I felt like corn syrup in his arms, and I knew if I stayed any longer, I'd be lying in a puddle either in the tack room or his bed. I had to create distance for both of us. I had nothing to offer Killian but my body, and he could get that anywhere. I needed to find out who I was before I let him determine who I should be.

"I'm not mad at you." In all honesty, I wasn't mad at him as much as I was frustrated with myself. My motivations weren't all that above board either. I'd let my body do the thinking. Wasn't it time to use my brain? "Your sweet talking isn't going to work anymore. I've been schooled. Those pretty words aren't getting you anywhere tonight, buddy. I'm heading to bed."

"I could tuck you in."

What little light there was in the stables glinted off his white teeth. His smile was as disarming as his personality. No girl was safe around him, especially me.

"I'm good, Killian." I was several feet away when I heard him tell Lucky in the end, he would win. However, I wasn't sure whether he was referring to winning over Lucky or me.

Back in the cabin, it was colder, the air mustier, and my future bleaker without the presence and sparkle of the big cowboy.

I struck a match and lit fire to the kindling Mickey had left ready a week ago. The smoke swirled and disappeared along with my hope up the chimney. The flames danced to the crackle and pop of the fire as I lay on the floor thinking about my future.

Thousands of thoughts whirred through my head, but they all came back to Killian and the beautiful moments we'd shared that week. I was determined to embrace those times as turning points in my life. Moments when a man shared his good points and revealed the good in me.

I slid my fingers under my shirt and traced the raised edges of my tattoo. If something so ugly could be turned into a thing of beauty, I could never give up on myself. A little voice inside of my head told me beauty could be found in everything, even a cowboy with good intentions and a bad history. Our friendship was worth salvaging.

Perception and reality were often so close in theory and so far apart in truth. Killian's need for control was simply a lie he told himself. We were all a bunch of liars, and somewhere buried deep inside was the truth.

I'd made it too easy for the man. I never put up a fuss or an argument. I let him have my body, mind, and my soul. In the past, I'd given in to everything because I'd had no options. I went to Tyler because I had no options, I went to jail because I had no options, I came to live at the ranch because I had no other options. In truth, most of my choices weren't driven by my lack of options, but my poor choices. Moving to the ranch wasn't one of them. My life was different now, full of options, full of decisions, and my toughest dilemma would be Killian.

I woke when the fire had died, and my body shuddered from the chill in the air. The orange glow of the sun reflected off the living room window. The quiet chirp of birds signaled the dawn of a new day—a new beginning.

When I arrived in the stables, Tyson and Cole were already hard at work. Killian was nowhere in sight.

"Where do you want me to start?" I pulled my pink gloves from the wall.

Cole walked out of Princess' stall. "You don't have to help; you've been cleaning stalls all week."

"I'm living at the ranch. Besides, I was hoping if I helped you two finish your tasks early, one of you could take me out driving. I need to get my driver's license soon so I can get a car of my own and not have to depend on everyone for rides."

"Killian doesn't seem to mind giving you rides," Tyson said, joining the conversation. I was pretty certain by the grins on their faces they weren't referring to anything that had to do with a vehicle.

After shaking my head in disgust, I addressed both men. "I am not going to discuss my riding habits. Now do you want my help or not? It's going to cost you a short driving lesson—in a truck, you dirty-minded men."

"I like trucks. Some of my best rides happened in my truck," Tyson piped in.

"I thought Killian was bad, but I swear, you two are worse." I pulled the wheelbarrow aside and walked toward the next stall. "Move out of the way unless you want to be wearing this shit."

"I'll take you as soon as these stables are finished. Any place you have in mind?" Cole stepped aside and let me enter the empty stall.

"Nope, just need to drive."

"I've got to make a small supply run, so you can take me there."

Tyson walked away from the conversation and led the miniature horse out to pasture.

"Perfect."

"What's perfect?" Killian, with his ghostlike approach, had snuck in behind me.

I leaped into the air at the sound of his voice. "Shit, Killian, do you have to sneak up on me?"

"I didn't sneak." He walked toward Lucky's stall. The horse had turned his cheek once again. "What's perfect?" He looked between me and Cole as if we were planning some kind of coup.

"Cole is going to take me on my next driving lesson."

"Like hell he is."

Cole and I both stopped what we were doing. I tossed the rake in the corner and walked toward Killian. I was done with his high-handed, bossy behavior.

"You are not going to control everything. Do you understand?"

I poked my finger in his chest. Lucky seemed to be very interested in this exchange. His head peeked over the stall door, and when the perfect moment presented itself, he lifted Killian's Stetson with a nudge and sent it flying in the air.

"You little bastard." Killian gave the horse a sour look. "Even the horses are siding with you."

I reached past Killian and stroked Lucky's head. "You're busy, so I'm bartering with Cole for driving time. I'll help clean stables, and he'll supervise my exemplary driving skills." I turned and looked Killian straight in the eyes.

"I could take you." Killian was acting like a child who'd just missed the ice cream truck.

"Yes, you could, and I'm sure I'll ask you again at some point, but for now Cole is stepping up so you can get back to work. You've been babysitting me all week. It's time for a break, don't you think?"

"I don't need a break from you, Megan. I like being with you."

He sounded so sincere, and I was sure he meant what he said, but I didn't want to continue to be this week's good-time girl.

Completely changing the subject, I turned the conversation to Lucky. "Is he getting Kill Camp today?"

"Lucky is getting saddled and rode today, whether he likes it or not."

"That should be fun to watch. Should I get a pillow and some ice for your sore ass?"

"Darlin', it's a rare day when someone doesn't want to be ridden by me."

The arrogant, sexy man turned in his boots and walked away. I believed his statement, though. Every woman I'd met last night would have gladly been the saddle for this man, regardless of what the outcome was. Every woman but me.

Chapter 18

KILLIAN

Lucky wasn't having anything to do with the saddle. The minute he saw it, he took off running in the opposite direction. It took me an hour to calm him down. We played our games for a while, then I tried again.

I stopped the minute I heard Cole's diesel truck start up. It didn't please me that Megan was alone with him, but she was right. I was trying to control the situation by controlling who was around her. I didn't like her needing other men. I didn't like it one bit, but I knew deep in my core I'd lose her if I alienated her from everyone. That was Tyler. I wasn't him.

Time seemed to stand still while Megan was gone. She brought a spark of energy to my existence. I loved to see her find herself in moments like today when she poked me in the chest. She was coming into her own voice and establishing her power in her new world. It was like watching a crocus break through the ground after a hard winter. The beauty of her unfolded like the delicate petals of a flower—a flower that survived the brutality of a lifetime of harsh winters.

What Megan didn't understand was she already belonged to me, but if she needed time to figure that out, I'd do my best to give it to her. I wasn't stepping aside, though. I would plant myself in her path so her only choice was to bloom through me. I wouldn't be the hard winter snow. I'd be the sun her petals yearned to touch.

Last night after she'd left me in the stables, I'd found her note on things she knew for sure. I was keeping it as a reminder that she had feelings for me. Right there on the middle of the page, it said, *Killian, is too sexy for my own good.* I'd make sure she knew I was everything that was good for her. Controlling? Maybe. Determined to have her? Definitely.

When the rumble of the truck echoed from the cabins, I let Lucky loose to run and hurried to where I knew Megan would be.

She was all smiles and giggles. Half of me basked in the glory of her joy. The other half bristled at the fact that I hadn't been the one to put that smile on her face.

She pulled several bags from the cab, the smell of burgers wafting across the air.

She watched my approach. "Oh, I'm glad you're here. I picked up lunch for everyone."

"Perfect, I'm starving. Your horse has been giving me a hell of a time."

"My horse?" With bags in hand, she wandered toward the hay bales stacked in front of the stables.

"Yep, he's sweet on you, so I think you should help train him. If you plan to be able to ride him, you'll need to be able to control him."

A little light of mischief glimmered in her eye. She looked over her shoulder toward Cole, who was twenty paces behind. Her head tilted toward me. "I rode you, but I'd hardly call you controlled."

Fuck me. I'd be damned if she wasn't getting all inside my head, and maybe a little inside my heart. "Some stubborn animals need a lot of riding before they can be deemed safe for the long-term."

"Is that right?" She pushed a bag into my arms. "I'll keep that in mind."

"Oh, it's definitely true. Lots of riding keeps an animal happy and satisfied."

"Are we still talking about the horse?" She grunted as she

climbed up the hay bale. I was tempted to grab her ass and give her a lift, but I refrained. Something told me that wouldn't be received well.

"Of course. What else would we be discussing?" I gave her what my mom used to call my Hells Angels look. It was all sweetness and light, but under the smile, the devil in me was lurking.

Cole dropped off the sodas and lingered, but one look from me told him to keep moving. He said he'd eat with Tyson in the barn because they had stuff to do there.

Smart man.

"So…" I popped a fry into my mouth and watched while she bit into her burger. "I thought we could work with Lucky together."

She nearly choked on her food until I handed her the soda.

"You can't be serious about making him my horse."

"Why not?"

"I don't know anything about horses."

"You live on a ranch, you gotta start somewhere. Besides, you know more than most people. What's more important is that you want to know, and you like them, and somehow you've connected with Lucky. I'd say that's enough for now; I'll teach you the rest."

"I don't know, Killian. Lucky is special, and he needs someone who understands his trauma. Someone who knows how to get him past it."

"He needs you. Who better to understand abuse than a survivor? Who better to coax him to recovery than someone on the same journey? I don't believe in accidents, Megan. I believe Lucky was brought here for you and you for him." *And you for me.*

"I don't know what to say."

"Don't say anything. Just have your cute ass in the arena in twenty minutes." I didn't give her the chance to decline. I grabbed my lunch and disappeared through the stable doors.

Giving her Lucky was a no-brainer. The damn horse looked for her all morning. He put up with me but was always looking sideways for her to appear. And if I was being honest with myself, giving her the horse was a selfish act because it would require her to be with me for hours at a time. I was determined to gain her trust.

Exactly twenty minutes later, she appeared dressed in her jeans, boots, and that sexy Stetson on her head. Every time I saw her, I felt a little twitch in my heart and a big one in my pants. I was acting worse than my pussy-whipped brothers. At least they went on with their normal routines. I manipulated the situation to keep her close.

Lucky lit up like a firecracker the minute she arrived. He ran around the arena with his mane and tail proudly on display. His trot became a walk when he rounded the corner in front of her. The damn bastard pranced in front of her like a show horse.

"Told you. You have the meanest horse on the property in love with you."

I opened the gate in front of her and led her into the arena. Lucky nudged me aside. He was basically telling me she was taken. He and I would have a heart-to-heart later.

"He's really a sweet horse." She ran her hand up his neck and threaded his mane through her fingers.

I knew what it felt like to have her fingers running through my hair. Lucky was named accurately this time around.

"Do you remember how I taught you to halter Sunset?" I held out the halter for her to grab.

"I do. You want me to put the halter on Lucky?"

"Well, I don't want you to put it on me."

She bobbled her head and rolled her eyes. A week ago, she would have been apologizing and flinching back in preparation for a punishment. Today, she wore her attitude like a badge of honor. That was progress.

Megan was a quick study. She had Lucky harnessed and ready to go in seconds. I would have sworn the horse harnessed himself just to please her.

"Now what?"

She stood to his left. I wasn't sure who looked more proud, the horse or her. They could have been entered in a best-of-show competition. I felt a sense of pride for having introduced them.

God, I'm a sap.

"Lead him to the center of the arena."

I followed close behind and instructed Megan on various exercises for her and Lucky to build trust, but honestly, they weren't needed. She had that horse under her spell as solidly as she had me; the only difference was, Lucky would remain in the stables while I would work on getting her back in my bed.

"The gang should be home soon," she said while she led Lucky around the arena.

I was happy to see my family, but on the other hand, that meant I'd have to share Megan with the others, and I was none too happy about that. My dad's voice echoed in my head. "Boy, control is a selfish habit. It's fine to have it, but it takes a bigger man to share it." That was the day he made me an apprentice trainer at the ranch. Since then, I'd been hanging on to my Irish pride and my sense of self like it was the last fiber connecting me to this life.

"I imagine they'll be here anytime. Should we give Lucky a rubdown before this place becomes a circus?"

"I think that's a good idea."

I stood behind Megan with her back to my front and walked her through the rubdown process. "Do you remember the first time we made love?"

She stiffened against me. "How could I forget the first time we had sex?"

I hated the way she emphasized the word 'sex'. "I'll never forget it either." It was burned into my brain. She was scared to death, but I spent the time needed to gain her trust. What a fucking amazing moment.

"Well, this is much the same. You're going to touch Lucky everywhere, and he's going to learn to trust your touch." I cradled her hand in mine and began to rub the horse around his shoulders. "Don't move too fast, and if you hit a sensitive spot and Lucky reacts, pull back and start again. Don't give up and let him win."

I let go of her hand and moved back a step. She moved slowly over the horse's back while I silently pulled out my camera and shot some pictures of her taming the beast. When she reached his hindquarters, Lucky sidestepped her touch. Megan did exactly as I'd asked her. She pulled away and started again, and in a few minutes her palm was gliding over the deep scars on his rump.

She moved with grace and precision around him like she'd been doing it for years, and short of the little apprehension Lucky felt at her touch on his scars, he seemed to love it, too. I snapped pictures of her throughout the process.

"Come here, Megan."

I pulled her toward me, and when she'd rounded the horse, I shot a selfie of me kissing her cheek. Her face was flush with happiness, and her eyes glowed like whiskey in the firelight.

"He let me touch him."

"Yes, and you let me touch you because you trusted me. Lucky trusts you." I was just about to make my move to her lips when the unmistakable sound of tires on gravel bounced off the walls of the arena. I wanted to groan, but I didn't—I controlled my reaction and smiled. "Looks like they're here. I'll take care of Lucky. Go see the girls."

I kissed the top of her head and patted her behind. She took off like a rabbit being chased by a fox.

Chapter 19

MEGAN

How was I supposed to be near Killian without wanting him every second? His hand was on my bottom for a fraction of a minute, and yet the heat from his touch seeped all the way to my core. Killian McKinley would be the demise of every piece of common sense I possessed. He jumbled my brain and set my body on fire with his presence. Add his touch, and I was a hopeless mess.

The girls were piling out of the truck when I got to Mickey's place. In less time than it took to inhale, I was pulled into their arms and whisked into the big house.

We sank into the soft seats in the living room. Holly and Mickey stared at me in silence.

"What?" I glanced around the room, looking for something out of place.

"Spill." Mickey pulled her legs under her body and relaxed into the arm of the plush brown sofa.

"You've just settled in like I have a novel to tell. I've got nothing to share."

Holly sank in on the other side of the sofa. They were sitting across from me like two detectives ready to grill me for my misdeeds.

"I gotta know." Holly fluffed up a pillow and shoved it under her head, a sure sign she was also in for the long version of the short week. "Is he awesome in bed?"

"Well, shit. Can't a girl keep something to herself?"

"No. Cellmates equals soul mates. Now spill your damn guts." Mickey's tone brooked no argument.

"It was the most fabulous experience of a lifetime, but it's over." My shoulders sank before I could hide the movement.

It was Holly's turn to yank my frail chain. "You are so full of shit. You are so not over it. Your eyes nearly fell back into your head when you thought about it."

"You were right. Killian is a player. I don't need that."

Mickey jumped off the couch and started for the door. "I'm gonna kick his ass for playing with your emotions."

"Mickey, stop," I yelled. She halted at the door and spun around. "He didn't mislead me. I gave myself to him, and he nurtured my soul."

"What the hell does that mean?" Mickey turned around, walked to the kitchen, and came back with three sodas. We popped the tops in unison.

"Hard to explain, but basically he showed me what life with a good man could be like. He made my body sing in a way I'd never known was possible. He made me feel valued, and he gave me the courage to move forward with my life." Killian had changed me. He'd set the bar high and low. He wasn't the keeper I'd hoped he'd be, so anyone who wanted monogamy would rank higher in that department, but I was certain no man could quench my desire the way he did.

"You've changed in the week we were gone. We left a scared girl and came home to a confident woman." Holly lifted her can. "Let's toast to the benefits of getting laid."

"I'd toast to that if I had a drink," Kerrick said as he entered the door with Keagan on his heels.

I knew my face turned red. I could feel the heat of embarrassment cover my skin. "Oh. My. God. Stop." I buried my face in my hands.

Mickey got up and hugged Kerrick. "You two are going to have to kill your little brother. He's been fondling my friend's heart." Back in the kitchen, she pulled out two beers and handed one to each of the brothers. "Just make sure you hide the body."

I came to Killian's rescue. "There will be no killing. Your brother was the perfect gentleman. He didn't take anything I didn't offer, and he made no promises."

I considered Killian's earlier statement about remembering when we made love. I would always remember it as a lovemaking session as opposed to simple sex, but I'd keep that to myself.

"We're happy to kick his ass for you. It would be just like it was when we were growing up."

Keagan kneeled before Holly and pressed his lips to her stomach. His touch was so loving and reverent, and I heard Killian's words from the other night: *I would have been on my knees in front of you kissing your stomach and thanking the heavens I had you and our child.*

"Oh my God, are you pregnant?" A lump lodged in my throat. "You are, aren't you?" I knew I should have reacted with joy, but my head was reeling from the news.

Holly's face went white. She frowned at Keagan and pushed him away from her belly. "I'm sorry, Megan. I wanted to wait to tell you, but my husband over here can't keep his hands off us."

I hid my hurt through lighthearted banter. "That's usually how people get pregnant. But it rarely happens with just hands." I squeezed between Keagan and Holly and placed my hand on her flat belly. "I'm so excited for you. Holy shit, I'm going to be an aunt." I smiled on the outside and wept within, but in spite of my pain, I felt happy knowing my friend was going to have a baby with a man who adored her and their unborn child.

The front door opened, and Killian walked in, followed by Tyson and Cole.

Killian tossed his Stetson on the entry table. "Who's knocked up?" He looked around the room, but his expressive eyes landed on me—and showed concern.

Again, I teased so the tears wouldn't flow. "Don't look at me. I haven't had enough sex to get knocked up." I gave Holly's tummy a final rub and took my seat across from them.

Killian came to stand behind me. "It only takes once, darlin'." His fingers danced across my shoulders. His presence and touch were a soothing balm to my abraded heart.

"I suppose since you're all standing in my living room, I should get a clue." Mickey looked around the room at all the cowboys. "I'll have your paychecks in a minute."

The group made themselves at home. In a way, this *was* their home. Much to Kerrick's disappointment, Mickey kept the house open for anyone who wanted to relax, and several cowboys and a bunch of women sure could raise a ruckus.

Over that noise, Kerrick shouted, "Pizza should be here any minute."

That simple gesture of making sure everyone was fed pulled me out of my moment of sorrow. Here I was at the Second Chance Ranch, surrounded by good people—salt of the earth people. How could I help not feeling like I'd found my golden ticket?

"Who can I persuade to give me a ride to the shelter tomorrow? I've decided to take their deal."

Cole and Tyson first looked at Killian. I couldn't see his expression because he was standing behind me, but from the looks on their faces, I knew he'd put a silent kibosh on any volunteering they might do.

Kerrick, Keagan, and Holly looked on in silence.

"I'll take you." Killian leaned over me. His voice was loud enough for my ears only. "Don't break my heart by saying no."

I'd gotten really good at my eye rolling over the past week. Killian had given me enough reasons to enhance that skill. "You're a piece of work, Killian."

"He's a piece of somethin'." Keagan stood up and looked at the bottom of his boot. "Typically, I'm scraping what he is off the sole of my shoe."

Fast as lightning and loud as thunder, two of the McKinley boys went after each other. Keagan and Killian weren't really fighting, just letting off some steam, but I'd never seen two grown men wrestle inside a house while the others looked on like it was entertainment.

Barbarians.

Mickey stepped over the men like they weren't there and began handing checks to the more civilized members of the group. Tyson tipped his hat and left. Cole folded his and stuffed it into his shirt pocket. "You want your check or not?" She waved the light blue papers in the air.

The men separated; Keagan sat his breathless body next to Holly while Killian scooted his hulk of a frame in front of my chair and leaned back against my legs. I was tempted to run my hands through his sweaty hair, but that wasn't something friends did. I needed to remind myself that Killian wasn't the best choice for me.

When Mickey handed Killian his check, she handed me one also.

"What's this?" I looked at the total and felt dizzy. I'd done laundry for years at the prison and didn't come close to making what Mickey had written on this check.

"Killian says you're acting as his assistant. As an employee of the ranch, you get paid."

"Oh no, I was just trying to earn my keep." I offered her the check, but she shook her head.

"It's my understanding you worked harder than that asshole Greer. Besides, Killian needs the help, and he's difficult to work with, so if you guys make a good team, then you've just saved me a ton of time looking for a replacement. You're hired. You report to Killian. He'll give you a wage review in three months."

By the way Mickey turned around, it was obvious she was done discussing it. I was officially employed, and I had a feeling Killian had a lot to do with the offer. I had no idea what I'd be doing from this point forward, but I'd be seeing a lot of Killian. That both thrilled me and terrified me. I felt like a kid in a bakery being told I could smell the goodies but not have them.

"Besides seducing my future brother-in-law, what else did you do while we were gone?" Mickey set the table while Kerrick went to the door to get the pizza, which had just arrived.

"God, does everyone have to know I slept with Killian?"

"Sweetie, there are no secrets at this ranch. The walls are too thin."

She was right about thin walls. Not a person walked in tonight without knowing what was being said on the other side.

"I met Killian's fan club. Did you know they call themselves the Kill Club?" There was no pride on Killian's face at the mention of his harem. "I also got a tattoo. Killian designed it."

"This I gotta see," Kerrick said. He dropped the four pizza boxes on the dining table. "What is it? A whip? Some cuffs? A ball gag?"

I shared a knowing look with Killian. I'd never divulge his secret. If he wanted to perpetuate rumors, then so be it.

"No, look at it." I slipped my T-shirt off my shoulder and exposed the field of flowers.

"Holy shit, that's awesome." Holly was at my back, tracing the flower petals and stems with her fingers while each occupant of the house admired my art.

Finally, Killian pulled my shirt back over my shoulder. "Let's eat. You can all gawk later." He guided me to the table and took the seat beside me.

I jumped when his hand slipped possessively over my thigh. It felt so perfect where it was, but I pushed it off. We weren't a thing. We'd simply had a moment—or two...or three—but that was over.

After we ate and cleaned up, I said my goodbyes to everyone and started toward the stables. I wanted to say goodnight to Sunset and Lucky before I climbed into bed. There was no telling what was in store for me tomorrow at the shelter.

Sunset was waiting for me, and after a few kind words and good neck rub, I moved on to my new man. Lucky leaned over the stall and brushed his muzzle through my hair.

"You got everyone fooled, you know. They think you're gruff and aggressive, but you're a sweetheart in tyrant's clothing. You remind me of a cowboy I know. He likes it when people are afraid of him, but inside he's the best man I know."

"Is that right?" Killian emerged from the shadows. "I couldn't help overhearing you speak of a cowboy you know. Anyone I'm familiar with?"

"You know you shouldn't eavesdrop on private conversations." I gave Lucky a pat and walked toward the door.

"I just wanted to check on you and see how you are handling Holly and Keagan's news."

"I won't lie and say it doesn't hurt, but I'm happy for them. I really am."

He stepped up next to me, and all I wanted to do was fall into his arms, but instead I turned and walked toward my cabin.

He raced forward and put his arm around my shoulders. "You know you don't have to avoid me. We're more than friends."

"I'm not avoiding you, and we are *only* friends, Killian. To be more with you means I'd be less of me." I broke away from his touch. "I'll see you tomorrow morning."

It took all I had to run to my cabin and lock myself inside. I wanted Killian, but I deserved more.

Chapter 20

KILLIAN

She left me standing between her cabin and my brother's. When I turned around, Keagan was laughing.

"Shut the hell up." I blew past him and into my home. It didn't stop him from following. "What the hell do you want?"

"I just want to sit back and watch you squirm. I never thought it would happen, but that woman has you all twisted up inside."

"Who's twisted up?" Kerrick pushed through the door, carrying a six-pack of beer and the leftover pizza.

"For a detective, you're pretty unobservant. Our baby brother is in love." Keagan threw himself into the overstuffed chair.

"I'm not in love. I'm in lust." I grabbed a beer from Kerrick and opened it on the edge of the coffee table.

"For a psychology major, you're pretty damned stupid."

My fists ached to shut their mouths, but I'd learned long ago that two against one never worked in my favor. "Unless you want your pregnant wife to be a widow, you better shut the hell up."

My brothers looked at me and broke into laughter.

Kerrick popped the top on his beer and handed one to Keagan. "Let's toast." He raised his bottle. "Here's to ex-cons and serving life sentences with them."

"You don't see a wedding ring on my finger or an engagement ring on hers, so leave it be." I took a long pull from my beer.

Keagan leaned forward and stared at my crotch. "Nope, but I see the rope marks around your nuts. She has you by the balls, and you're not man enough to admit it."

I sucked down the rest of the beer and grabbed another. "All right. I like her. A lot. I'm not ready to propose or race her down to City Hall. I simply want to spend more time with her. Explore the possibilities."

"So what's the problem?" Kerrick pulled a floppy piece of pizza from the box.

"She doesn't want me."

Beer squirted from Keagan's nose. "She cockblocked you? That's the funniest shit I've ever heard."

"Shut up. She doesn't think I'm sincere in my desire to be with her, but I plan to prove her wrong."

"Let's hope she's not as stubborn as you. With breeding starting in a few months, I can't have you distracted."

"I'll be all right. Mark my words, she'll be back in my bed within the week."

They both stood and walked to the door. "Sometimes you're more ego than common sense." Kerrick patted my back and pulled Keagan from my cabin.

The thing about family was, they never beat around the bush. They saw what I refused to acknowledge. What I felt for Megan was about more than sex. We had a connection. In the week I'd spent alone with her, I knew more about her than any woman I'd ever been with. I could tell you her favorite coffee, soda, ice cream, and TV show. I knew her scent, the feel of her skin. I could diagram every dimple, freckle, and scar. Who was I kidding, I had fallen for Megan Connelly—hard and fast—and I'd stop at nothing until she was mine.

THE TRUCK WAS RUNNING and warm when she emerged from her cabin looking far too pretty for the shelter. In her hand, she held an unopened soda and an orange.

"Mornin', darlin'." I opened her door and helped her inside. Last night, I'd come up with a plan: I'd woo her back into my life; I'd earn her respect and trust. "I made you a lunch."

I handed her the plastic bag that contained a turkey sandwich, a bag of chips, a soda, and the marshmallow treats I'd picked out from the box of Lucky Charms. Given my time constraints and the lack of planning, I thought I'd done pretty well, but plastic bags and candied marshmallow pieces wouldn't cut it the next time. If I wanted to win her heart, I'd need more preparation. Once I dropped her off, I'd be hitting the grocery store.

"Thanks for the lunch and the ride. I'll try to get a lift home."

"No way. I'll be there. What are friends for if not to lend a hand?" No fucking way was she getting a lift home. Any lifting of Megan would be done by me.

"Okay, I should be finished by four."

"That's perfect. I thought we'd put a saddle on Lucky and see if he'll let you ride him."

She pivoted in her seat and stared at me, slack-jawed. "You're kidding, right? He won't let *you* ride him. What makes you think he'll let me?"

"I've got a feeling Lucky would let you do anything to him. I won't put you in danger. I just want to try something out. Sound good?"

A little spark of something flashed in her eyes. "Sounds good to me."

I shouldn't have glanced at her. When she slid her wet tongue over her bottom lip, I swerved and nearly hit the car beside me. What did she do? She laughed. Somehow, some way, she would pay for that.

The parking lot in front of the shelter was nearly empty when we pulled up. I rushed to open her door and help her out. My mother would be proud. Like a schoolboy with a crush, I carried her lunch and soda to the door, where she was buzzed in and we parted.

I was pleased to see they had some type of security protocol. Four years of studying the human psyche meant I knew how crazy love and possession could make a person. These women might be in a shelter, but they were far from safe. The minute they walked out that door, they were targets.

It took all I had in me to start my truck and drive away. I already felt lonely. This would be the first day I wouldn't be spending with Megan.

When I walked into the supermarket, I approached my shopping with intent. Usually I'd run in and grab milk, cereal, and a few staples like hot dogs and burgers, but today I looked at everything with one question looming in the background: would Megan like it?

I put several bunches of daisies in various colors in my cart and pushed toward the produce aisle.

"Hey, there." Trish planted herself in my path.

The last thing I wanted was to deal with her. She was the catalyst of all my woes with Megan. "What's up, Trish?" I reversed and moved around her, stopping at the strawberries. I knew it was too early in the season, but these came from South America and smelled sweet.

"What did I do to cause you to lose interest in me?" She grabbed my cart and halted my progress.

I wanted to tell her I was never interested in her, but I knew that would be painful for her to hear. "Trish, we had fun. We gave each other what we needed and moved on."

"I didn't move on." She tugged at the miniskirt that had ridden too far up her thighs. "I always liked you more than you liked me."

I didn't want this to play out in the middle of the produce department, but there was no other way. "I never led you to believe we were more than a hookup. I thought we had an understanding."

"You had an understanding. I had a dream."

Holy shit. Megan was right. You couldn't sleep with a woman repeatedly and expect her to feel nothing. I'd lied to myself for so many years, I'd believed it. My truth was that if I didn't get involved, I couldn't lose control.

"Trish, I'm sorry. I never meant to hurt you." I shuffled my feet and waited for her to release my cart.

"You know what hurt the most?" Tears pooled in her eyes. She tilted her head to the ceiling. "When I walked out of Greer's cabin that morning and saw you with Megan, you looked at her in a way I had hoped you'd look at me. There was love in your eyes. I hated her, and I envied her."

I stepped around the cart and pulled Trish into a friendly hug. "I really am sorry, Trish. For a man who studied human behavior, I sure didn't consider mine."

I released her and stepped back. Trish was pretty. She had a wild spirit and warm heart. I'd overlooked those qualities.

"Do you love her?" She wiped at the smudge of glistening mascara under her eyes.

"You know what? I think I may, or at least I could." To verbalize the truth was liberating. I'd accused Megan of lying to herself over and over again when I was doing the same. "What about you and Greer?"

Trish held her hand to her head like it was a gun and pulled the thumb trigger. "He's a big asshole with a tiny dick."

"Glad you figured that out early on."

"I figured a lot out that day." She flipped her hair back and stood tall. "I have more value than a simple roll in the hay. I'll never be anyone's leftovers, and seeing the way you looked at Megan made me realize I could find that, too, with the right man."

She was right. There was a man out there who could love and cherish her. I wasn't that man. My heart was wrapped up in a little ex-con.

I stepped around my cart and pulled her in for a final hug. "Never settle for less than you deserve."

Trish gripped my shirt and breathed me in like it was her last breath, then she pivoted on her heels and walked away. Trish was not the only woman I'd been with who wanted more. Many apologies were in order.

Chapter 21

MEGAN

The morning whizzed by with introductions, a review of policy and procedures, and a short talk from the director. It turns out my counselor had something to do with this deal. Apparently, she thought I had a lot to offer young abused women, since I'd been through it, and I would make a good listener. And that's what I did all morning. I listened.

A pregnant nineteen-year-old named Sarah told me how she'd run away from home at seventeen and lived in her boyfriend's treehouse in the forest. She became dependent on him, and he liked that control. She gave up school because anyone she talked to would get her in trouble. I knew what that kind of trouble felt like. It revealed itself as a cast on Sarah's right arm.

I knew how another person's control turned me into a little and insignificant person. It was probably the one thing that scared me about Killian. His need for control meant I would lose mine, and I wouldn't give a man that type of control ever again.

April was thirty and had four kids hanging from her waist. Lined up, they could have been stair steps. The poor woman was kept knocked up and beat up. The bruises on her face were light green

Set in Stone

and yellow—externally almost healed, but internally a festering wound.

Mona was the one I worried about the most. She was perky and pretty, and on first glance I'd never guess she'd been abused, but that only meant it had happened for so long that she was good at hiding it. She had no bruises or broken bones, which meant her scars went deep.

My fingers unconsciously sought out the tattoo on my back. Tyler was responsible for my wounds, but Killian was responsible for my healing. How could he be so perfectly imperfect?

At break time, I went next door to grab a mocha latte and brought the sack lunch Killian had made me. Inside was a turkey sandwich with the crust cut off, a bag of chips, and a bag of the marshmallows from Lucky Charms. Wrapped in foil to keep it cold was my favorite soda. How could I not fall for a man who cut the crust off the bread and picked out the candy hearts, stars, and moons from a box of cereal just for me?

I whipped my phone from my pocket. It had been buried all day. In spite of never having held a job, I had a good work ethic. Somewhere ingrained in me was the motto "Always do your best." Even though I wasn't getting paid for my work at the shelter, I didn't feel it was right to be on my phone all day.

The first thing that lit up my screen was a message from Killian.

Your horse misses you.

Attached to the message was a picture of Lucky, or rather Lucky's ass end. I would have to break him of that bad habit. Killian had saved Lucky, and he deserved more respect. Killian had saved me in a lot of ways, too. Was I judging him too hard? Did we both misunderstand his need for control? Maybe it wasn't control he was after. Maybe it was respect.

I typed out a quick text.

I miss being there. Thanks for the lunch, Killian. You're the best male friend a girl could have.

The best friend, the best lover, the best—

A man approached my table. "Hey, I haven't seen you here. My name is Mike, and I own the place."

Reluctantly, I set my phone down. Rude wasn't in my makeup. Maybe it should have been all along, but if someone took the time to talk to you and they were polite, then I imagined they deserved my full attention.

"Hi, Mike. I'm Megan, and I'm volunteering next door."

A look of understanding came over his face.

"They go through a lot of volunteers over there. I imagine it's a stressful position. Watching those women breaks my heart. I wish I could help."

"Feeling sorry for them doesn't help them. Giving them a job or an ear could be beneficial." I sipped at my mocha latte and glanced at my phone. No response from Killian.

"Most of them won't come in here because it's owned by a man." He bent over and picked up a napkin from the floor. Mike was tall and good-looking. Not handsome like Killian, but cute in a computer-nerd way.

"Do you want to be a Good Samaritan today?"

"What did you have in mind?"

"You want to donate some cookies and hot chocolate for our one o'clock sharing session?"

The center provided the necessities, but it was obvious its budget was stretched thin. Diapers and staples would always come before treats. One thing I knew was a little kindness and a cookie could go a long way toward earning trust.

"I could do that. Do you want to pick them up?"

"No, you should bring them over. Meet the women who are living next door."

Mike nodded and disappeared to round up the treats.

I watched my screen for the rest of my break to see whether Killian would reply. His lack of response made me wonder whether I'd pushed him too far away.

At one, Mike buzzed the door and I let him in. Men weren't a welcome sight at the shelter, and as I walked him through the hallway, the women pressed themselves into the walls to let him pass.

He set up the drinks and treats on a side table and started for the door.

"Before he leaves, I just wanted to say thanks to Mike from The Big Brew next door. He generously offered to supply treats for this week's meeting."

The children's faces lit up. One thing I knew from my time in prison was that the way to a woman's heart was through her children, or if there were no children involved, through chocolate.

Nods of consent came from several women. The children took off for the treat table like a bull from the chute. They all ran for the cookies, with the exception of one small boy who grabbed Mike's hand.

"Thank you, Mr. Mike. I love cookies almost as much as I love my mommy." The little boy looked at his mom sitting in the corner. "See, Mom, some boys are nice."

Mike's shocked expression couldn't come close to that of the woman who smiled and opened her arms to hug her boy.

Mrs. Vega, the shelter director, introduced me to the women again. Then she proceeded to applaud them for getting away from their abusers. The group talked about how easy it was to return to the scene of the crime. It was familiar to them, whereas their new future was uncertain. That was when the counselor asked me to share my story.

After a short description of what happened to me, I closed my story with this. "I know what it feels like to run and be pulled back in. I also know what it feels like to be desperate. I acted out of desperation to save my unborn child, and I failed, but I did save myself, and my future is unwritten."

Mona stood up and yelled, "You should be glad you lost your baby! Why would you have wanted to have a monster's child?"

She stunned me with her words, but I had an answer. "It was my child, too. I wanted to protect anything that was beautiful in that life. In the end, the universe had a different plan."

What shocked me more than Mona's outburst, though, was my ability to talk to a bunch of strangers about my loss. A week ago, I never would have been able to do that; I was barely able to share my conviction with the ranch crew, let alone the circumstances surrounding it. Today, I was stronger and wiser. I owed some of that confidence to a sexy cowboy who showed me what it felt like to be valued and heard.

At four o'clock, Killian was standing outside the shelter, leaning against his truck. His Stetson was on his head. His legs were crossed comfortably in front of him, and his hands were wrapped around a bunch of daisies. My heart caught in my throat.

"Hey, darlin'." He kicked off the truck and walked to me, thrusting the flowers into my hand. "These aren't as pretty as you, but I thought they'd be nice."

The daisies didn't smell like much, but I brought them to my nose anyway. Having spent time in the truck with Killian, the flowers had taken on his citrus scent.

"They're beautiful and so thoughtful."

I tiptoed up and tried to place a kiss on his cheek, but he turned his head and I caught his lips. A look of triumph covered his face. He looked a hell of a lot like Lucky right then.

"You're driving." He held out his hand and dangled the keys.

Snatching at the keys, I pulled them from his fingers. "Did you have a rough day and now have a death wish? You realize the route home requires a trip on the freeway, right?"

"I trust you. You are totally capable. Besides, you have a horse waiting for you, and I figured that would motivate you to get us home safely."

He said 'home' like we lived together. I knew there was no meaning to the words for him, but I liked the sound of it anyway.

I white-knuckled it when we were on the freeway and breathed easier once we hit the country road that led us back to the ranch. One glance at Killian, and I was tempted to crash his truck. His smirk was unforgivable. While I was battling for our lives on I-25, he was making fun of my granny posture.

When we pulled up in front of the cabins, he scooted over on the bench and began to peel my grip from the black leather wheel.

"Relax. Your fingers are stuck so tight, I may need a crowbar to pry them off the steering wheel." Once he had extricated me from the black wheel of death, he massaged my hands. "I didn't want to break your concentration while you were driving, but I did want to know how your day went."

"You called me a granny."

"You looked like an old woman huddled over the dash. Relax."

I loved the gentle way he always got me to unwind. His touch was like a magic elixir for my frazzled nerves. In a weak moment, I leaned against him and exhaled.

"The day went remarkably well. It's sad to be on the other side. I looked at those women and saw myself in various moments of my life. Then some girl told me I should be glad to have lost my child. I was shocked at first. I never considered my baby to be anyone's but mine." I burrowed my head into his chest and hoped he would wrap his arms around me, but he didn't.

"You have a heavyweight horse waiting for you to saddle him up and ride him." Killian was getting good at pulling me from places I felt compelled to cling to—my past—my guilt—and him.

"Are we heading to the tack room?" I knew I shouldn't tease him, but then again, he *had* compared me to a geriatric driver.

"We do, but it isn't for what I'd like to do there. It's for getting the equipment you need to ride Lucky." He reached over me and opened the driver's door. In seconds, he was walking to his cabin. "I'll meet you there in ten."

I watched him walk away from me. The jeans he wore hugged every muscle of his backside, something my hands had gripped to pull him inside me, and now with every step, he was getting farther from my reach.

After putting my daisies in water, I changed into ranch wear and raced to the tack room. When I arrived, the room was empty. On the wooden horse sat the blanket Killian had laid me down upon and made my body quiver.

"Grab a pad, the hackamore, and the brush. I'll get the saddle."

He had snuck up on me while I was reliving the past. I had been at the part where his head sank between my legs when he pushed his way into my thoughts.

I followed him into the arena, where Lucky was tethered to a pole in the center. When he saw me, he pulled at the rope as if to close the distance.

Chapter 22

KILLIAN

She was going to be the death of me. I had to grab the saddle and hightail it out of the tack room. I loved control, but I could only tether so much of it when it came to Megan. Seeing her lost in her thoughts as she stared at the blanket had me thinking how amazing it would be to have her under me right then. I was ready to crawl inside her body and live there, but she made the point that she needed to find herself, and I couldn't argue with that. I only hoped when she did find herself, I was part of the picture.

"I want you to brush him down, especially where we are going to place the pad. He's going to sweat, and a sweaty back is a slippery back. Getting those loose hairs off will help him be a stable ride." I handed her the brush and turned away to adjust my jeans.

She approached the horse with care, doing exactly as I'd taught her. She made her presence known, not that the horse missed her entrance. The stubborn bastard spent his days looking for her.

Bridling Lucky was like harnessing energy. Once he acquiesced, I showed her how to get him to move in the directions she chose. She had to control him, not the other way around.

He responded to her like she'd trained him from birth. She

moved, and he watched. I'd never been more proud of a horse or woman in my life.

Once the saddle pad was in place, I had her walk him around to get used to the feel. When I approached with the saddle, all hell broke loose. Lucky reared, and my heart fell into my stomach. He rose on his hind legs above Megan, threatening to crush her. Just as I was getting ready to pull the reins from her hand, she gave me a five-fingered stop.

"Wait. He's scared." She cooed and spoke softly to the big horse until he settled down and buried his muzzle into her hair. "It's okay, boy. No one here will hurt you."

"Maybe this wasn't my best idea. I've tried to saddle him, and he's not amenable to the idea. Let's give him some space and time."

"No, he'll be okay. He's just scared. Do you remember the first days when I was here and I flinched when you came near? You didn't give up on me. You didn't back away. I'm not giving up on him. He doesn't need time; he needs the right touch." She pulled the reins, making sure she had control of Lucky's head. "Come here, boy." She pulled him to where I'd dropped the saddle.

"Megan, I don't want you to push him too far. He's dangerous."

"Let me try, Killian. When you were acclimating me to your touch, you didn't completely back off. You took a breath and tried again, and that's what I'm doing. If I walk away, he wins."

I couldn't argue with her. I would have worn the horse down a bit, too, and tried again. I just didn't want to see her get hurt.

"Go slow and approach with care. I don't want you flat on your back unless I'm kneeling between your legs."

Shit, open mouth and insert boot.

As if she didn't hear me, she leaned over and hefted the saddle into her arms. It wasn't light, but she pulled it off the ground like it was nothing. With the reins in her palm and the saddle in her hands, she hoisted it onto his back. He shifted and settled, then sidled up next to my girl. Yep, Megan was a natural.

"Now what?" She stood with her shoulders back and her head held high.

I was shocked she got the saddle on the big oaf. The damn horse looked at me like he was pleased with himself. Anyone who says animals are stupid hasn't got an ounce of sense. Lucky was one-upping me and winning.

"Let's tighten the saddle and let him get used to it. No riding today. I think a few more rounds of putting the saddle on and taking it off will be good."

And so she did. Over the next hour and a half, she saddled and unsaddled him three more times. When she removed the saddle for the night, Lucky happily followed Megan to his stall.

"I have dinner for us." I carried the saddle into the tack room. She was hot on my heels. "Roasted chicken, potatoes, and garlic green beans."

"You made dinner?" She hung up the bridle and laid the pad over a wooden horse. "For me?"

"In all honesty, I can't say I cooked it myself, but I purchased it with you in mind. I was hoping you'd join me." I wasn't good at this dating stuff—didn't have the faintest notion of how to go about it. I was more of a get-in-and-get-it-on kind of guy, but with Megan, I needed to wind it back and make a fresh start for us. There was no future if I couldn't remedy the past. All those women I'd had fun with had made sure of that.

"Come here." I lifted my arm around her shoulders and guided her into my cabin. The table was set for two.

"Pretty confident, aren't you?" She yanked off her boots and tossed them in the corner.

"I'd say hopeful, not necessarily confident." When Megan arrived, she brought something special to my existence: a feeling of completion. Corny as it sounds, she was the A to my B.

I pulled the food from the oven and served it up.

"Can I work with Lucky during my lunch break tomorrow?"

"You can work with him whenever you want."

"I'll get my work done first. I'll be in the stalls at five." She sucked butter off a green bean; the action was so innocently seductive. She had no idea of the power she had over me, and I had no intention of telling her. "It wouldn't be wise to disappoint the boss."

"I can think of all sorts of ways you can please the boss."

It was never a good sign when a woman's eyebrows shot up to her hairline. "I think we need to talk about this thing between us."

Damn straight we did. "I agree."

"Oh good, then you agree our decision to be friends is the best one to make?"

Oh my God, the friend card again.

"Megan—"

"Hear me out...we had a great time. I learned a lot about myself last week, and I'm grateful for the lessons, but I can't be that girl for you. Besides, you're now officially my boss, and fraternization never goes well for the underling."

"Fuck that. Keagan sleeps with Holly, and he works here. Kerrick sleeps with Mickey, and she owns the place. She sets the precedent." I'd make a bad litigator.

"Kerrick is a detective, and Holly works for a nonprofit. They are hardly employees of the ranch."

"This is bullshit." I felt her slipping away with each passing second.

"It may be bullshit, but it's the way I need it to be. What happens if I don't sleep with you? Do you fire me? Make me sand the rails? Fix the fences? I can't give you that kind of power over my life." She flopped back and crossed her arms over her chest.

"I'd never do that. You and I are separate from the ranch."

"No, we're not. We live here, eat here, and work here. We are as connected to this ranch as the scrub oak out front." She slid her chair out and picked up her plate.

"Sit down, Megan. We're not finished with this discussion." I pulled the dish from her hand and placed it to the side. When I reached for her, she stepped away.

"Here's the problem, Killian. If you get your way, I lose everything. I'm just getting used to being me. I've never been in control of anything, and I want to know what that feels like. Surely a man with such a desire to control everything around him can understand."

"I don't want to control you. Hell, I can barely control myself when I'm with you." The truth didn't faze her.

"You may not want to control me, but you do it anyway. It's in your nature to control what you can, and I won't be part of that mix. Thanks for dinner, Killian." She picked up her boots and opened the door. She looked over her shoulder. "I'll be in the stables at five." Then she was gone, and I was left with an ache in my chest so painful, it felt like she'd kneed me in the heart.

Chapter 23

MEGAN

As long as I could remember, my life had been tough, but pushing Killian away was by far the hardest thing I'd done. Deep in my heart, I knew he was a good man. The problem was, I couldn't risk everything just to have him. I needed this cabin, this job, and my friends. And getting involved with him would put everything at risk.

In the quiet of the morning, the winter wind whirled between the cabins, kicking up the dusting of snow that fell last night. The temperature wasn't a deterrent. I'd felt colder tossing and turning all night in my bed. I'd hurt him; that was obvious by the fallen look on his face when I walked out of his cabin. When I'd walked into mine, the warmth he'd brought to everything disappeared.

First to arrive at the stables, I went through the morning routine I'd learned from Killian. First I checked on all the horses, then I gathered the equipment. I separated hay, filled the nets, and started on the cleanup. Cleaning stalls was mindless work. I raked and shoveled my way through several stalls before anyone showed up.

Cole entered the stables first. "Mornin', Megan."

"Yep, it's morning all right." I swiped at the bead of sweat that was running down my forehead.

"Killian put me in charge of you today. He'll be working in the barn with Keagan, getting ready for breedin' season." Cole pulled on a pair of gloves and took the wheelbarrow from me. "Mickey will be off getting sponsors for the junior rodeo we are hosting this spring, so Killian wants you in the tack room, oiling saddles and cleaning gear."

"I'll do whatever you need me to do." Lucky nickered as I walked past his stall. In a funk, I hadn't stopped by to see him. "I'll be back later." My mood was as dark as his mane.

The smell of lemon oil filled the room. With a flick of the switch, the bare bulb sputtered to life and lit up the dark corners. Saddles of every size and color sat like riders on wooden horses. Leather reins, halters, and harnesses hung neatly from hooks on the wall. Training sticks lay on the table, and in the corner sat the blanket where Killian and I had made love. Sitting on top was a single yellow daisy. Nerves fluttered in the pit of my stomach.

After Cole had shown me how to care for the leather, I got to work. The morning ticked past in snippets of memories. Short little reminders of the things Killian and I had done or said since the beginning. While I mindlessly oiled the saddles, my mind relived every moment I'd spent in Killian's arms. Moments I'd cherish and never forget.

"Time for lunch." Cole startled me. How these men moved around silently dumbfounded me. They were all over two hundred pounds of chiseled granite, but they walked through life as silent as a whisper. "You've got an hour, and when you get back, we're going to ride a few of the horses. Killian wants them exercised."

"Where is Killian?"

"Not sure. I think he's in the wood shop. He usually goes there when he needs time alone." Cole spun on his boots and left me alone in the tack room with my thoughts and my daisy.

Lunch was spent eating a yogurt and sipping a cup of hot chocolate. The self-help book sat there, mocking me. What now? What now? Well, I didn't have a flippin' clue.

What I knew for sure and the lies I told myself were all behind me; the next assignment was personal affirmation. I needed to write five positive things going on in my life.

I am alive.
I have choices.
I have a job.
I have a horse.
I've had Killian.

My last entry was more of a reflection rather than a positive affirmation. I scratched through it and wrote my last entry.

I have friends.

Holly was just pulling in when I was walking back from lunch. "Where have you been?"

"I'm still volunteering several days a week at the hospice center." She rubbed at a red splotch on her white shirt. "Today, I brought sugar cookies to Mrs. Lakely. She's in the final stages of lung cancer. She invited her granddaughter, and we decorated heart-shaped cookies for Valentine's Day. Her granddaughter Sadie was liberal with the frosting and sprinkles." Holly shook her head, and a few colored sprinkles landed on the ground in front of her. "Are you okay?"

I didn't want to burden her with my issues, especially since I wasn't sure of what my issues were. All I knew was I was surrounded by people, and yet I'd never felt more alone.

"Of course. I'm good. Didn't sleep well last night. Just tired."

I was tired. I'd never managed my life before, but it was exhausting work. I couldn't blame anyone else for my decisions. No one could take credit for my successes or failures but me.

"Go grab that big cowboy you like so much. I'll bet you he can wake you up." Holly headed for her cabin, where, I imagined, her own big cowboy was waiting for her.

WHEN FRIDAY ROLLED AROUND, I was ready to let off some steam. Killian had pulled a disappearing act, but I knew he was around by the daisies he'd tucked into the crack of my porch swing or left lying in the wheelbarrow.

I had to give him credit. He was giving me space to find myself, and the only thing I knew for certain was that I felt less without him. His exit from my life had left a gaping hole where want, hope, and desire resided. It didn't help that I'd begun to dream of him, of his lips against mine, of his arms wrapped around me in a solid embrace. I missed him.

He'd made Cole my supervisor so I had no interaction with him when it came to the ranch or the work I was asked to perform. He still controlled everything, even from afar, but I realized it was for my health and safety.

I'd been chomping at the bit to ride Lucky, but Cole kept me busy riding the other horses under the guise that they needed exercise. In truth, Killian was making sure I found my seat. Building my skills as a rider was necessary when it came to Lucky. His unpredictability could have gotten me injured or worse.

I hoped I'd see him tonight at Rick's Roost. When I told him I didn't want to be a part of the mix, I never meant I didn't want him in my life. He and I definitely needed to talk.

After another lonely lunch with my book and my yogurt, I met Cole in the arena, where I assumed I'd be giving another horse exercise. To my surprise, the only horse around was Lucky. Cole was trying to brush him down. Lucky had other ideas.

"I'll take care of him. He's particular when it comes to his grooming. He likes a gentle touch."

"Get him brushed down, because we are saddling him up and you're riding him today."

"Really?" I snatched the brush from his hand and made quick work of removing the loose hairs. I'd worked tirelessly getting Lucky used to the saddle. He'd trusted me enough to care for and nurture him.

"Yep, Killi...I mean, I think you're ready." Cole traded me the brush for a saddle blanket.

A herd of buffalo ran through my stomach, rustling up my insecurities. Was I good enough, worthy enough, brave enough? Where was Killian when I needed him the most? He should be here watching me ride Lucky for the first time.

"Where's Killian?"

"He's around."

He was always around. I could feel him despite the fact that I couldn't see him.

"Saddle him up, and I'll give you a boost." Cole leaned against the rail and watched me heft the saddle into place. I marked off a checklist in my head as I tightened the cinch strap, checked the hackamore, and grabbed the reins.

"I'm as ready as I'll ever be. Any words of wisdom?"

Cole checked my rigging. "Make sure you stay in control the whole time."

The word 'control' came up a lot at the ranch. It seemed to be an attribute everyone was after. Including me. Was Killian so wrong to want it? Was I wrong not to relinquish it?

I stepped into Cole's woven hands, and he boosted me up and into the saddle. Lucky stamped his hooves and sidestepped until I pulled him back to where we started. My voice seemed to settle him. Soft and slow, I reminded him we were friends, and I prayed this wasn't the day he decided to change his mind about me.

"What do you want me to do?" I adjusted my seat and shortened the reins in my grip.

"Walk the rail. You determine the pace and direction. Remember, respect is earned, not given, especially with a stubborn horse like Lucky."

I pulled the reins to the right and walked Lucky around the first turn. He picked up his pace, and I pulled him back. He was responsive to my touch. Suddenly, the air changed in the arena and I knew Killian was somewhere. Lucky hugged the rail, at times crushing my leg into it.

"Take him out a few feet. Don't let him do that to you."

My heart stilled at the sound of Killian's voice. Gruff and impatient, but there. I pulled Lucky to the left, and we stayed on that path until we rounded the corner. Killian was sitting on the rail, watching me. His expression was hard to read. Pride twitched in his eyes, but there wasn't a smile on his face. His lips were stretched into a thin line.

I pulled Lucky to a stop in front of him. "I've missed you. Were you avoiding me?"

"Pretty much, yes." He hopped off the fence and approached Lucky.

His honesty lanced my chest. "You don't have to avoid me. We're supposed to be friends." Lucky picked up on the emotions welling in my chest. His first reaction was avoidance. Sidestepping, he created distance between Killian and me. Little did the horse know, I'd dug a wide trench already.

"I can't be your friend, Megan, when I want so much more. Don't ask me to accept less than what I want."

"Can we talk about it?"

Was this the end of everything? Would he dismiss me completely? Walk out of my life for good? I gripped the reins without thought and crossed my arms in front of me.

Lucky decided at that moment to be a disobedient horse. He reared up and unseated me. I slid off the back of the saddle and landed flat on my ass, staring up at Lucky's butt. Not a vision I'd recommend to anyone.

In seconds, Killian had Lucky tethered to the rail, then he was by my side.

"Are you okay?" His hands roamed over my body. "Are you hurt?"

If all it took was a fall from a horse to get Killian's attention, I would have gladly sacrificed myself a week ago.

Was I hurt? I took inventory of my parts and decided I'd live to see another day in the saddle. "No, I'm okay, but Killian, we really need to talk. I don't want to have to resort to acrobatics in order to talk to you. This isn't a circus."

He pulled me to my feet. "Back in the saddle you go." Instead of offering me a lift up, he watched me put my foot in the stirrup, and when I attempted to hoist myself up and failed, he cradled my ass in his hands until I took my seat. "I gotta run. We can talk later."

"But—"

I was talking to air.

Chapter 24

KILLIAN

She wanted to talk to me, and I left her with a bruised ego and no doubt a bruised ass. There was no way I'd stand around and let her tell me all the reasons we could only be friends. I didn't want to hear it, especially when I knew it wasn't true. She wanted space. I gave her space. Space that nearly killed me each day she walked past my cabin.

When I wasn't thinking of her, my time was spent with Keagan in the barn. We'd moved everything out and retrofitted it with foaling stalls. Three beautiful babies would arrive in the summer—two colts and one filly. We were ready.

I needed to get this thing with Megan resolved before spring, but before I could talk to her, there were three women who deserved a sincere apology. I headed to Rick's, hoping to see the trio before the ranch gang arrived.

Like clockwork, Carrie, Maggie, and Gabby arrived at five o'clock, decked out and ready to rock some cowboy's world.

"Hey, ladies."

Carrie was the most vocal of the three. "What do you want, Killian?" She brushed past me on her way to the bar.

I'd known this wasn't going to be easy, but I hadn't anticipated being met with such disdain. I followed the three to the bar. "I want to talk." I analyzed the group, hoping for a break in their steely exterior. "I'll buy the drinks if you'll listen."

Five minutes later, we were sitting in the same booth Megan and I had shared when everything went to shit.

Carrie spoke while I poured the girls a beer from the pitcher I'd purchased.

"We're only sitting here because you're buying the drinks, so you better talk fast or plan on buying another round."

"I wanted to apologize."

Carrie dropped her beer, and the four of us were bathed in dark brown stout.

Gabby piped in next. "Mr. Go In for the Kill is apologizing? What for? Killin' it?"

I gripped my hair, wanting to pull it out by the roots. "I'm sorry I played with your emotions. I thought we were on the same page. I was wrong."

Their silence was deafening. To fill the space, I kept talking.

"I never meant to hurt any of you. I thought we were having fun."

Maggie picked up the pitcher and refilled Carrie's beer. "I don't know about you two," she said, looking at her friends, "but I was using him for sex." She lifted her shoulders and graced me with a passing glance. "It was great sex, but you were simply a dick with a dick."

Ouch! "I deserved that." I flagged down the waitress and asked for another pitcher of beer. "Look, I was an ass, and I want to make amends."

"How do you plan to do that?" Carrie drew pictures in the condensation on her mug. "Are you volunteering to be used for sex?"

Was that hope I saw in her expression? "Um…no…"

I didn't really have a plan. Apologizing was as far as I'd gotten in my outline to right my wrongs. Using sex as a way to be forgiven for using them for sex was never going to happen.

Maggie piped in, "That's a shame. I was hoping for a little relief from all the heartache you've caused me." She'd really missed her calling. Best supporting actress for a drama would have suited her better than working at the mall. "I suppose I'll settle for a dance later, and another pitcher of beer."

I had felt Megan before I saw her. She was energy mixed with the warmth of the sun. Sandwiched between Mickey and my two brothers, she walked into the bar and scanned the room. Her eyes settled on me, then shifted to the three women in the booth.

Carrie craned her neck to watch Megan disappear down the hall to the restroom. "You two are quite the thing, aren't you?"

Megan was moving faster than an angry stallion. The door at the end of the hall slammed so hard, the walls rattled.

"I gotta go." I tossed two twenties on the table and left. I needed to set things straight with Megan.

Chapter 25

MEGAN

Hiding in the bathroom wasn't going to solve my problems. Was it really only a couple of weeks ago I was looking into this same mirror, giving myself a pep talk?

I stared at my reflection and wondered out loud, "What is Killian's game?" Seeing him sitting with the Kill Club didn't sit right with me. He was up to something. Power? Control? Manipulation? It was Killian, so if it was one, it was probably all.

How could he make me feel so special and at the same time confused? The horse. The tattoo. The daisies. Then there was the Kill Club, the manipulation, and then avoidance.

Maybe that was his game. He charmed me with his sweet words and melted my heart with his smile. Was I special? No. I was just a part of the non-exclusive group known as the Kill Club.

My heart sagged with the weight of the truth. I gave him my body. I gave him my trust. I gave him a piece of my heart. But the one thing he wanted, I couldn't give him—control.

I splashed my face with water and allowed myself one more moment before I pulled back my shoulders and braced for the night ahead.

I ripped open the door and walked into a wall of muscle. With a tilt of my head, I was staring into endless pools of blue. Killian had the eyes of an angel, with the disposition of the devil.

"Sorry. I'm so sorry." My shaky fingers skimmed the front of his shirt and gripped the material for stability.

He leaned in, caging me between his arms. "No need for apologies, darlin'."

I released the bunched-up cotton gripped between my fingers and gulped in a breath of courage. "Back to stalking?"

"Guilty as charged. I've told you before, long, dark hallways are dangerous."

"Yeah, well, I told you I could take care of myself."

"I could take care of you, Megan, if you'd only let me."

"Is that right?" I ducked under his arm and yelled back over my shoulder, "I think it's cute you think so." This conversation mimicked our first—only this time I was in control, or at least pretending to be.

Killian scowled and leaned against the far wall for the next half-hour. His eyes never left me while I nursed my beer in silence. When Holly and Mickey left me alone to dance, Killian pushed off the wall and stalked toward me like he was a hunter and I was the prey.

"Let's dance."

"Are you asking or demanding?"

"Dance with me, please."

"Only because you said please."

"My meeting with the trio is not what you think." He pulled me close to his body despite the upbeat tempo of the music. "Megan, I was apologizing to them. You opened my eyes. Don't you get it? I'm not interested in them. I'm interested in you."

It felt too good to be in his arms, and staying there would only confuse my heart. I needed to replace emotion with logic. Sadly, nothing about Killian was cut-and-dried.

"You are so much more to me. You have no idea the power you have over me." His grip on my shoulders was a cross between desperation and the determination to control me.

The song ended, and another began. "Come home with me and let's talk. It's too loud in here, too many people."

"Where were you when I wanted to talk earlier? Oh…that's right. You were controlling the situation. No, Killian." I pushed away from his chest. "Not interested." The light in his blue eyes dulled. "Listen, I don't want to be your enemy. Let's just agree to be friends."

I was halfway across the room when he spoke, "I don't want to be your friend. I want to be your everything."

Had I imagined those words, or did he actually say them? It was hard to tell over the noise of the crowd. When I turned back, he was gone.

No one at the table mentioned Killian's absence or my foul mood. It would have been great to drown myself in alcohol, but I was the designated driver. Wednesday, Holly was taking me to get my license. In several paychecks, I'd have enough money to get a decent used car. I was finally taking the reins of my life.

Last night's whipping wind had been a warning of things to come. While we were hanging out at Rick's, two inches of snow had fallen. The ground was white except for the two tracks that led from where Killian's truck had been parked.

Cole took the men while I chauffeured the girls back home. Adopting my granny posture, I vowed to get them home unscathed.

Mickey was more interested in answering a text than getting in Holly's Jeep. "Did you and Killian have a fight?" She darkened the screen and tossed her phone in her bag.

"No, we came to a mutual agreement." I reached down and turned the defroster on high.

"I'm calling bullshit on that." Holly rubbed her sleeve against the fogging passenger side window.

"I told you guys it was over. Killian and I were simply defining a path forward."

Mickey turned in her seat. I couldn't see her expression, but the air around us was filled with tension. Unhappiness had an energy all its own. It was heavy and damp, and it soaked into your soul.

"Does that path have something to do with why I just got a message that he'll be in Wyoming for a few days?"

"What?"

Set in Stone

Mickey pulled her phone from her bag. She lit the screen and pressed it in front of my face.

"Stop it." I pushed the phone aside. "I'm trying to drive here." I hunched over the steering wheel and proceeded to drive at a snail's pace through the snow.

Holly pulled the phone from Mickey's grasp. "It says, 'I have some stuff to take care of. Cole, Tyson, and Megan have the horses under control.'"

"He's leaving?"

"Yes, and he doesn't mention when he's coming back. Damn it, Megan. You guys have to figure this out."

"There's nothing to figure." I drove under the swinging Second Chance Ranch sign.

"I was going to kick his ass for playing with your emotions, but now I think I may have to kick yours for screwing with his. That boy is in love with you."

"Yep, he confessed as much to his brothers last week." Holly leaned over Mickey and held my hand. "He's got it bad for you."

My foot slipped off the gas pedal. The truck came to a full stop several hundred yards from the cabins.

"No way. He's an asshole who uses women for sex. He moves from one girl to the next without thought of what that does to the women he's discarded."

"He's a McKinley, and that name comes with arrogance and bravado, as well as stubbornness and stupidity. But it also comes with a vulnerability he'll never show you. He'll bleed out before he lets you know you've delivered the fatal blow." Mickey pointed to the men waiting in the distance. "Do you think it was easy for them? They're stubborn Irish men. They were in control of everything until we showed up. It's scary for a man to realize everything he is and everything he'll be is found in the eyes of a woman." Mickey patted my leg and stared ahead. "Do what's right for you, but I'll tell you this, you can never go wrong with one of them."

The last hundred yards were the hardest to navigate. Tears clouded my vision while his words filled my heart.

I don't want to be your friend. I want to be your everything.

Chapter 26

KILLIAN

The farther I got away from the ranch, the clearer the picture had become. I'd totally fucked it all up this time. I'd found the one, and I'd lost her. In the same way I'd let the world think I was this whip-wielding control freak, I'd allowed her to make up her version of our truth.

I straightened her crumpled note on the steering wheel and rolled it over to the part that read, *Killian isn't what he seems.* Nope. I was better than what I'd showed her. I wasn't giving up; I was gaining distance and perspective.

Several times, my phone chimed with an incoming message. Cursory glances showed several messages from my brothers and Mickey. But then one single message was from Megan.

I'm sorry.

I pulled over to text her back.

Me too.

I needed some enlightenment, and there was no one more qualified than my mother, Katherine McKinley. She'd either whip me into shape or whip my ass. Maybe both. All the while, she'd be making my favorite meals of lamb stew and soda bread—comfort foods for a wounded spirit.

Set in Stone

I couldn't ghost into the ranch with the way my truck tires crunched along the gravel drive. On the porch was my mother, wrapped in her pink robe and slippers. She folded me into her arms, and for the first time in two decades, I cried. The last time I'd let my tears spill, I was eight and my yellow Lab had passed away. Like many of the horses I had trained, Barley was a rescue I'd adopted from the local humane society. He was six when I took him in, and he lived as long as he could for me. We'd been inseparable.

"I've got tea ready. Keagan called and said you were on your way. Let's talk."

I had recently been schooled on the meaning of that phrase. Those words meant you'd better plant your ass and pay close attention because A) you would be quizzed later, or B) your life was about to change. Maybe both.

"Tell me about her." Mom poured tea while I listed off at least a hundred amazing things about Megan, from her resilience to the tiny freckle above her right eye.

"Mom, she's been through a lot in her life. She's been bossed, and bullied, and beat."

She pulled a tin of cookies from the cupboard and passed two my way. "Well, if she can survive that, she can survive a McKinley. The McKinley women have to be tough as nails, son, or we'd never survive our men. One thing I know for sure is, I raised my boys to be strong, to do the right thing, and to love deeply. Show her those qualities, and I'm sure you'll win her back."

"I don't know what the next step should be." I had no clue how to proceed.

"Call her, and tell her you love her. Turn off your phone and let her chew on that thought for a week."

She spoke as if she had some experience in the matter. "Is that what Dad did to you?"

"No, baby. It's what I did to him. When you leave them with love, it only brings longing. Let her really miss you." She swooped the empty cups off the table. "Your room is ready." She ruffled my hair and disappeared down the hallway.

I paced in front of my parents' barn. *What if she doesn't answer?*

What if she doesn't care? I gripped my hair and pulled at the roots. Losing her wasn't an option.

It took three rings for her to answer. Her breath was uneven and wispy. By the sound of horses in the background, she was already in the stables.

"Killian—"

"Wait…please don't say anything. There's something I have to say first. You wanted to talk the other day. I didn't know how to say what I was feeling. I'm going to say it, and then I'm going to hang up. Not because I don't want to hear what you have to say, but because I don't want you to respond until you've had time to process the information."

I inhaled courage and exhaled the truth.

"I love you, Megan. I love everything about you, and that scares the hell out of me. You unsettled my world when you arrived. I lost control of my focus. I couldn't get a handle on my emotions. Yes, there were other women before you, but there will never be another. You're it for me. What you have to decide is if I'll be too much or not enough for you."

I didn't want to give her time to respond. If she told me she loved me, I'd be racing back to her arms today. If she told me it would never work, there was a good chance I'd be burying my face in my mother's robe. So, I continued without stopping.

"I've got to go. I'll see you in a week or so. I left you something in the tack room. I love you."

Pressing end was hard. I tucked my phone into the pocket over my heart.

Chapter 27

MEGAN

He hung up. He declared his undying love for me, then the phone went dead. I redialed his number, but the call went straight to voicemail.

Typical Killian. He'd control the situation and get the last word in. I was enraged and euphoric. Two ends of the spectrum of emotions all bottled up in a moment.

He loves me.
Everything about me.
There will be no other.

I dropped the rake and ran to the tack room. On the blanket were a single yellow daisy and a stack of boards tied together with twine. Except they weren't boards; they were picture frames handmade from old barn wood, sanded to perfection. Each photo he'd framed was a snapshot of my journey to this moment.

The first was a picture of me in the stables. By the lack of light, it must have been taken at night. Lucky's head rested on mine. We both looked tired and scared.

The second picture was of me grooming Lucky. It was the moment just before I'd touched his scars for the first time. I'd approached him slowly, with gentleness and compassion, much the same way Killian had approached me,

A lump caught in my throat. Killian was still touching my scars. The ones no one could see. Insecurity. Shame. Helplessness.

The final picture was the one Killian took when he kissed my cheek, and right there I could see what I couldn't before. He loved me. It was in his eyes. They glistened with hope and passion.

I hugged the frames to my chest and cried. Hadn't I railed at him, telling him I'd never allow him to control me? I'd have to take back those words. Killian never demanded control, but I'd unknowingly given it to him when I fell in love.

Your submission would be the greatest gift because then I'd know you trusted me.

After getting his voicemail several times, I gave up trying to call him. I'd asked for space once, and he'd given it to me. The least I could do was respect his needs.

Monday was depressing. Holly drove me to the shelter, where I found out Sarah had returned to her abuser.

Wednesday offered a temporary highlight: the moment I walked out of the DMV with my driver's license in hand.

The rest of the days were spent in the stalls or the arena riding Lucky. I'd even ventured out on the trail, but Mickey insisted she accompany me. I told her about Killian, and all she gave me was an I-told-you-so smile.

Nights were spent working through the exercises in the self-help book. I was on the last chapter when I realized I really had learned a lot about myself—and the world—on the *What Now?* journey.

Being honest with myself is the first step in being honest with others.

People aren't always who they appear to be. Sometimes a deeper look is necessary.

Free will is something that can't be taken away from you. You might be trapped in body, but your mind and spirit will always be free.

Lessons come in many forms, like the horse that taught me about perseverance and patience.

Love can be found in the strangest places. The petal of a daisy, the smell of lemon oil in the tack room, or the blue eyes of a stubborn cowboy.

Set in Stone

MORE THAN A WEEK HAD PASSED, and if it hadn't been for the daisies being delivered daily, I would have thought Killian had forgotten me. *I love you* was inscribed on every card delivered. Those words were all I needed, but the text that arrived one morning was even better. It said, *I'm coming home.*

Holly dropped me off at the shelter on her way to work. When I arrived, Mona was in the conference room with Mike. They were setting out cookies and hot cocoa for the Monday group session. Their innocent little touches and bursts of laughter filled my heart with hope and happiness.

All day long, I watched the clock. At three-fifty, my sexy cowboy climbed out of his truck and leaned against the door. He adjusted his hat, rolled up the sleeves, and tugged on his belt buckle.

Every cell in my body tingled.

Ten minutes.

Damn it.

Fuck it.

I clocked out and ran toward my future. "Killian." The sound *ugh* whooshed from Killian's chest when I threw myself into his arms. We didn't exchange words; we exchanged love in the form of kisses and hugs. When we parted for a breath, his words floored me.

"I love you, Megan. You walked into my life and took control of my heart. I'm helpless without you."

Maybe I had been wrong about control. It wasn't always what it seemed; sometimes it was simply a way to steer someone towards a different path. In my case, it led me to love.

Next up is *Set Up*

A Sneak Peek at Set Up

Diamonds are a girl's best friend...so they say. That's true until they're analyzed, picked apart, and declared flawed—or jailed for grand larceny.

"Natalie Diamond. I can't believe they're letting you go."

Officer Ellis stood behind the out-processing counter and greeted me with a beer belly and tobacco-stained smile.

"You're going to miss me."

All I had to do was flash my ten-carat smile and lean in their direction, and the other guards were charmed—but not Officer Ellis; he didn't fall for a peek of cleavage. Of course, with a prison-issued bra, a girl couldn't get the lift it took to gain the notice she deserved, but a nice word and smile could gain you favor, and favor was what you wanted when you were stuck in a cellblock with a bunch of bitches.

Officer Ellis always had a smile to share.

He licked his sausage-like fingers and shuffled through a stack of papers two inches thick until he found the one with my name typed across the top. "In the grand scheme of things, you were easy, young lady."

"Now, Officer Ellis, don't be starting rumors about me."

He shook his head with fatherly disapproval and slapped my exit form on the counter. "Honey, I don't need to start rumors about you. The whole place has been buzzing with them for years." He rocked back and forth while he tapped the computer keyboard with furious urgency.

I'd given the guards a run for their money, but I'd been taught to make my mark on society. There was no way to leave here and not be a legend. I was Natalie Diamond, and that meant I was made to sparkle.

"How fast can you spring me from this joint?"

"You in a hurry?" His pudgy digits raced over the keyboard. With that much movement, his fingers should be thin and sleek, but Officer Ellis' wife loved to bake, and he loved to eat. On occasion, my brand of sparkle would earn me a double chocolate brownie.

"Yes." I pulled at the pencil skirt three seasons out of fashion and tighter than a pair of Spanx. Those brownies had not been my friend. Sweets managed to go straight to my ass.

"Big date?" There was that fatherly look again—the one that pulled an honest answer straight from my soul.

"As a matter of fact, I'm going to see Mickey, Holly, and Megan."

He growled something inaudible. "That has trouble written all over it." He cleared his throat. "I better not see you in here again. Your dad might be gone, but if you show up in my cell block again, I'll stand in for him and turn you over my knee."

"Oh, Officer Ellis." I lowered my head and lifted my eyes. "Don't tease me." Coy was a hard look to pull off when my face was free of make-up. A girl was supposed to look through the fringe of her lashes to set the tone, but Maybelline hadn't made its way to the commissary of this facility.

"Natalie, get your life together. Figure out who you are."

A female officer entered through a side door and plopped a plastic bag on the counter, then turned and walked back through the same door without a word or a look. To her I was invisible. A number. A nobody. One fewer body to cavity search.

"I'm whoever I need to be. That's the best way to be in order to

A Sneak Peek at Set Up

survive in this world. Today I'm a Diamond, and I have those four *C*s in my pocket. I'm the epitome of quality."

That line was my mantra. One that had been played on repeat my entire life. *Believe it and conceive it*, my mother always said, but believing and conceiving didn't make it true—it just perpetuated whatever lie was being told.

Officer Ellis' laugh echoed off the faded gray walls. "You've got the four *C*s down all right. Cute. Cunning. Creative. Chameleon."

Yep, Officer Ellis had me pegged. That's probably why I liked him so much. He saw me for who I wasn't. During my lifetime of twenty-five years, I had tried on more personas than an A-list actor, but in the past three, I had never fooled him.

I plucked a behavior straight from my fussy teen arsenal and rolled my eyes skyward. "You're such a comedian."

He stamped the outtake form with the date and opened the plastic bag, dumping all the contents on the counter.

"Look through it and sign here." He pointed to the bottom of the page.

I signed without looking. It didn't matter whether everything was there. What I had was three years old and in dire need of replacement. But my heart skipped a beat when the gold tube of Cardinal Sin lipstick rolled toward me, begging to be applied. A signature color was important branding for a girl. If you had to be known for something, red lipstick was a start. A turn of the cylinder and stroke across my dry lips, and suddenly I felt more like myself. It was funny how the cloak of a little lipstick could make me feel authentic.

I reached inside the Coach bag, and my fingers brushed against a slim piece of fabric. It was still there. My heart leapt.

I pulled the red satin ribbon out and curled it in my palm. My mind reached back to before this terrible, cold, gray place to before the bad decision, to before my path went left instead of right.

To when my father was still alive. I could see him, on his knees before eight-year-old me, sliding the ribbon off the box and tying it to my wrist.

Be a good girl, sweetheart, and good things will happen.

I'd kept the ribbon all these years. A reminder, a talisman. For a long time, I'd lost track of the message in that slender scrap, but now I vowed, as I looped the frayed ribbon around my wrist, now I would remember.

Be a good girl, sweetheart, and good things will happen.

I needed some good in my life.

"I'm serious, Natalie. I don't want to see you back here." Office Ellis' voice was tinged with warmth and sadness. He once said I reminded him of his daughter. She was a lucky girl to have him for a father. He was a simple man, but a good man. It showed in his belly laughs and gifted brownies.

I stood tall and gave him a salute. "Yes, sir, but if I were to come back, just know it wouldn't be because I stole my own stuff and got caught doing it."

"Yeah, yeah, three years later, and you're still claiming innocence." He tucked the completed form into a drawer beneath the computer screen.

"No, I took it, but I was taking something that rightly belonged to me."

He shook his head. "Keep telling yourself lies, and you'll always be imprisoned, whether it's here or in your head." He pointed to the door. "You staying or going?"

"Going." I shoved the rest of my stuff into my bag and waited like a child to be dismissed.

"Get the hell out of my prison, Natalie Diamond, and never come back. You're better than this place. Find your purpose."

"My purpose begins with a trip to Cherry Creek Mall. I'm going shopping." I knew my strengths. That was something I could be a very good girl at.

Another shake of his head, and he pushed the button that opened the door to my future. My heart hammered when I touched the handle. What was waiting outside? My mother, I hoped, or maybe her driver, or Rosa the housekeeper. Mickey had offered to pick me up, but I needed to clear the air with my mother. I'd sent her my release date and time weeks ago; surely, she'd be here.

In a hurry to be free, I pushed the door and swung it wide open,

A Sneak Peek at Set Up

hitting the metal rail behind it. It popped back, and if not for quick reflexes, I would have been knocked flat on my butt.

Spring air whipped around me, fresh and crisp. Off to my right was the yard, the place I'd spent most mornings and late afternoons dreaming of freedom. I breathed deep. It was the same air, but somehow today smelled different. Freedom carried its own scent.

The sun sat high on the horizon. Streams of light pierced my eyes like lasers. Squinting through the glare, I searched the parking lot for a familiar face or car, but only an old, beat-up brown sedan was present.

I swallowed the lump of despair lodged in my throat and searched the area one more time, hoping I'd missed something. At the bottom of the steps stood a little blonde girl dressed in a pink tutu and shiny black shoes. One look at me, and her bright smile curled south into a frown.

"It's not her, Grandma." She stomped her Mary Janes and crossed her arms over a T-shirt that read 'Mama's Girl' in purple glitter.

"She's comin', baby. We're early." The older woman tugged at the little girl's pigtails.

"We should have brought her flowers."

Her little voice fell with every word, like somehow her presence would be less if she didn't bring gifts. Maybe that was my problem. Would Mom have shown up if gifts were promised? I was the damn gift. Didn't she understand that?

"We can't afford flowers, honey. We was lucky to get here at all." The older woman looked back at the brown car held together by body shop putty and duct tape.

Slumped against her grandmother, Little Miss Sunshine sighed. The breeze carried her disappointment to my ears.

I made my way down the metal stairs, taking each step carefully so I didn't catch a heel in the grate. When I got to the bottom, I stood in front of the munchkin.

Her head tilted back until her blue eyes stared into mine. "Do you know my mommy?"

"Who's your mommy?"

A Sneak Peek at Set Up

I looked past her and craned my neck in the direction of the road. Nothing. Not even a wisp of dust lifted in the distance.

"Del White." She said the name with pride, like everyone should know her mom.

It didn't sound familiar, but there were hundreds of inmates, and it was hard to be sure. "Sorry, I don't recognize that name." I looked over my shoulder toward the metal door. "It could be a while. The system works on its own time, but she'll be here." A little smile tipped the edge of her mouth. "I heard you talk about flowers." I looked to the right, where wildflowers danced in the breeze against the yard fence.

"I wanted flowers for Mommy, but we can't get 'em." Her little shoulders sagged like a tired old woman's.

"This could be your lucky day." I pegged Grandma with a look and nodded toward the fence. "Can we?"

Once she acquiesced, I held out my hand, and a sticky little palm slipped into it. "How old are you?" She lifted her free hand and showed me five fingers. "Wow, five. You're almost old enough to drive."

She giggled and skipped while I struggled to walk in my four-inch heels. It was bad enough that I was out of practice, but with all the holes and pebbles in my path, I was lucky to stay on my feet and not face plant onto the asphalt.

Grandma followed closely behind, not taking her eyes off little blondie. She didn't need to worry—the little girl was darling, but if I were going back to prison, it wouldn't be for kidnapping.

"Oooh," the little sprite whispered when she noticed the wild daisies growing along the chain-link fence.

"Go wild, little one."

I let go of her hand and stood back. She raced ahead and danced along the prison enclosure, picking the white and yellow flowers without reserve. When she finished, she had no less than a dozen stems spilling from her hands.

She struggled with the bundle, which needed something to bind the stems together.

"What's your name?"

"Emily."

"Well, Emily, take a look around and see if you can find a hair tie or a ribbon."

A brief glance around the parking lot came up empty. The little girl's eyes zoomed in on the red ribbon I'd wrapped around my wrist.

"Not this one, honey. It's my lucky ribbon." I rubbed the frayed satin.

"What makes it lucky?" She was as cute as one of those little capuchin monkeys—the ones that steal your heart—then your wallet.

"It was given to me by someone I love."

"Emily, we better let this woman get on her way." Grandma bent over to pick up several dropped flowers.

Those two were a pair. They could've made a mint on any corner with a sign that said, "I'm cute—give me whatever you got." Only, this little girl wasn't asking for anything. All she wanted was to show her mom she loved her by giving her a bunch of hand-picked daisies that would be withered and dead within an hour.

I took one last look at my lucky ribbon. It was a child's reminder of the love of a parent now gone. Did I need a reminder of Daddy's love? At twenty-five, did I need his memory telling me to behave? I'd lived without it for the past three years; surely, I'd survive now. Besides, it hadn't been lucky for me when I got arrested, but maybe Emily would feel lucky to receive it.

I slid my fingers over it one last time and said a silent *I love you* to my father before I unfastened it. "Now it's your lucky ribbon. Take care of it, okay?"

With great attention to detail, I tied the perfect bow around the stems. Emily's gap-toothed smile made another appearance, and I knew I'd made the right decision. To me, it was a reminder of the past. To Emily, it was a harbinger of her future—an offering to her mother that contained dreams of a new life, and I hoped it was a happy one.

"Thank you."

She brought the daisies to her nose and inhaled. If her grin was any indication, they didn't smell like dirt the way I imagined. Emily's smile made it look like they were scented with sugar and hope.

Just then, the metal door to the prison swung open and that little blonde monkey bounded away from me and into the arms of her mother.

It didn't take much for them to race to the beat-up car and zoom away, leaving me alone and wondering why my mother didn't love me enough to show up.

Get a free book.

Go to www.authorkellycollins.com

Other Books by Kelly Collins

The Second Chance Series
Set Free

Set Aside

Set in Stone

Set Up

Set on You

The Second Chance Series Box Set

The Boys of Fury Series
Redeeming Ryker

Saving Silas

Delivering Decker

The Boys of Fury Boxset

About the Author

International bestselling author of more than thirty novels, Kelly Collins writes with the intention of keeping love alive. Always a romantic, she blends real-life events with her vivid imagination to create characters and stories that lovers of contemporary romance, new adult, and romantic suspense will return to again and again.

For More Information
www.authorkellycollins.com
kelly@authorkellycollins.com

Acknowledgments

No book gets written without the support of family and friends, and a slew of amazing people like cover designers, editors, and proofreaders.

I could never live without my priority reader team, and the dozen or so proofreaders who volunteer their time to read my work.

I am humbled each time someone buys one of my books and leaves a review. Thank you dear reader for your continued support.

Hugs,
Kelly